Bloody Knuckles

A Tranay Adams Novel

CW01496967

BLOODY KNUCKLES

BLOODY KNUCKLES

CHAPTER ONE

Big Daddy's was a gentlemen's club that was frequented by those who came from all walks of life. Dirty and legit money flowed through the place. The employees nor the owner cared about this. As far as they were concerned, money was money. It all spent the same. The club was lit by neon green, blue, purple and pink lights. These arrays of colorful lights lined the walls, entrances, exits, bar, and stage. The exotic dancers' makeup, lipstick, tattoos and even contact lenses glowed.

Big Daddy's had some of the most incredibly beautiful women, natural and enhanced, but equally lusted after. There were ladies serving food and drinks as well as soliciting lap dances and sex in what they'd nicknamed *Heaven's View*. That was where all of the sucking and fucking went down. For the right price a trick could turn his wildest fantasies into a reality.

Thirsty men with hard-ons whistled and cheered for the phenomenal beauty putting on a show on stage. The phenom that had everyone's attention was Chrissy, but she performed under the moniker, Chris Swallows. The youthful temptress was a brown-skinned, five-foot-four joint with more curves than the number eight. She wore a curly 30-inch bussdown with blonde and golden-brown highlights and white contact lenses that made her look like the undead. She licked her abnormally long, pierced tongue at her adoring fans and outstretched her arms. She moved her body like a belly dancer while the

Caucasian anaconda slithered around her, in sync with her hypnotizing movements.

The tricks surrounding the stage threw money at her like it was useless. They watched her candidly while she watched a man partially hidden in the shadows. They eyed each other hungrily while he took the occasional sip of his drink and allowed a topless caramel-skinned chick to grind into his lap. Chrissy didn't know why but seeing him with another woman turned her on to no end. She could literally feel her pussy clenching and unclenching like a fist. Her nipples became elongated and rigid. Her breathing became labored. She found herself shuddering and her knees weakened. There was something about the way he was looking at her that made her feel like he was fucking her savagely, right there on stage in front of everyone. She tried to fight off her arousal for as long as she could, but she couldn't take it anymore. As soon as the song ended, Chrissy jumped off the stage and retreated to the women's restroom. The man that had been watching her, sat his glass down on the table, dropped a twenty on the caramel honey and chased after Chrissy.

He found her waiting for him holding the women's restroom door open. As soon as he entered, she removed her black leather coochie cutters and slung them aside. While she was occupied locking the door behind them, he unbuckled his jeans and stepped out of them. He had one leg in them so he kicked them off. He took off his boxer briefs and exposed what the Lord had blessed him with. It was thick, covered in veins and about seven inches long. Chrissy feasted her eyes on all that meat and licked her top lip. A clear gel oozed out of his peehole and toyed with the idea of falling to the floor.

Homie mad dogged her like she was an opp as he pumped his brick. She didn't know why but the sight raised her arousal to levels she didn't know existed. She wanted him so badly she had thoughts of ripping open the flesh of his chest and wearing his skin like a jacket.

"Goddamn, Jayvon, I want you so fuckin' bad! Look at—look at my—my pussy, bae. It's jumping and leaking and shit," Chrissy told him, looking down at her womanhood while holding its lips open. Sure, enough her sex was jumping and expelling its essence.

"Damn," Jayvon said, enticed by her treasure. He licked his lips and continued to pump his brick. "I want chu bad too, Doll."

With that, Chrissy pounced on him like a bloodthirsty vampire, and he caught her under her thighs. He carried her over against the wall as they made out. The sounds of their saliva sloshing around, and heavy breathing filled the air. She sunk her teeth into the warm flesh of his neck and started sucking on it. The sensation made him groan and grimace. He could literally feel his piece growing harder with anticipation of caressing her insides. While she nibbled on his neck, he swept his mushroom tip up and down her steaming, wet opening before he pressed his full potential into her. Chrissy threw her head back gasping. Her eyes flipped to their whites and her mouth hung open. She locked her ankles around his waist, just above his hairy buttocks. He sucked on her tits as he pounded her out. She held the top of the stall's wall and massaged her clit.

His animalistic grunting had her orgasm building to epic proportions. Her eyes grew wider and so did her mouth. Her pretty white painted toenails curled in her black stilettos. She whined and shook. He kissed all over her chest, and even on her breasts where his name was inked "Jayvon".

"Oh, my God, baby, don't stop! Please, don't stop!" Chrissy shouted. "I'm cuming, I'm cuming, I'm almost...I'm almost there! Oh, God! Oh, God! Oh, God!"

"Haa! Haa! Haa! Haa! Haa!" Jayvon breathed heavily, piping Chrissy harder and faster.

"Somebody is in there fuckin'," a girl said from the otherside of the door.

"How you know?" Another girl asked.

"Because I can hear 'em, bitch. What do you think?" The other girl replied.

"Well, I got the bubble guts and gotta shit so these mufuggas gon' have to come out! Y'all move out of the way," a third girl added before banging at the door.

"I'm so close, babe. I'm so fuckin' close! Don't stop! I swear to fuckin' Christ if you stop, I'ma stab you through your heart with the bottom of my fuckin' stiletto. Ooooooooh!"

Jayvon laid into Chrissy like he was trying to fuck her head off her shoulders. She lay the back of her head against the wall. Her eyes turned over to their whites again and her mouth quivered. Jayvon's grunts filled the air along with the girl's banging at the restroom's door. Abruptly, Chrissy came back alive, looking at Jayvon like he was attempting to murder her while her legs trembled terribly. She tried to say something but the pending orgasm had her choked up.

"Yeah, yeah. That's what I'm talkin' about! Look at that face, look at that fuckin' face! This pussy is mine, all mine! I own this muthafucka! Right? Right? Right?" Jayvon growled and bared his teeth.

"Yeaaaaah!" Chrissy cried, shaking uncontrollably. As soon as she orgasmed there was a splash below her. She lay against the wall limply as Jayvon continued to fuck her brains out, working vigorously toward his nut, ignoring the continuous banging at the door.

"Ah, ah, yeah, here I cum! Shit! Shiit! Shiiiiiit!" Jayvon hollered, unleashing his warm, wet babies deep inside of her womb. He continued to grunt and pump until he'd emptied his balls completely. He then laid his sweaty face against Chrissy's chest. He panted out of breath as she closed her eyes and rubbed the top of his head. Listening to her heart beat, he imagined he was an unborn baby again, in the safest place he could be in the world, his mother's womb. Where he didn't have to worry about food, shelter, paying bills—none of the things adults have to worry about now.

The banging at the door again brought Jayvon back to the present. He realized he was inside the women's restroom in the strip club with his girlfriend, Chrissy.

"Bae, where the hell were you just now?" Chrissy grinned, holding his face in her hands.

"I don't know. I guess I was wiggin'," Jayvon replied with a grin.

"Lemme get cleaned up so these aggy ass bitchez can use the shit house." Chrissy headed to one of the stalls to piss out Jayvon's babies and freshen up. She walked past the restroom door but doubled back. She banged on the door and shouted back at those on the other side. "You hoes chill the fuck out! You can use this muthafucka once I'm done!"

The banging at the restroom door continued despite Chrissy's rant. She rolled her eyes as she walked away to take care of her hygiene. Jayvon took the time to wash his dick and balls in the sink. He put his meat back up and buckled his belt. He was in the middle of washing his hands when Chrissy emerged from the stall behind him. She washed up and dried off then they headed for the restroom door.

"Yo, open up this goddamn door, 'fore I kick this mufucka in!" Earthquake's voice boomed from the other side of the restroom door.

Chrissy unlocked the women's restroom door and the women poured inside, rushing over to the stalls to relieve themselves. Chrissy and Jayvon were standing before Earthquake, one of the club's bouncers. He was a meaty head nigga, standing six-foot-five with cornrows, a five o'clock shadow and goatee.

"Chrissy, I know good and goddamn well you and yo' boyfriend wasn't in here slappin' skins," Earthquake said. He kept his eyes glued on them as he moved out of the way to let them pass.

Chrissy grinned as she led Jayvon out of the restroom by his hand. "Hmmph, wouldn't you like to know."

Earthquake watched as Chrissy and Jayvon disappeared down the hallway. Shaking his head, he made his way down the corridor behind them. "These hoes and their lack of respect for this establishment."

***

Chrissy sat at a table full of money she'd accumulated that night popping her pussy. She counted the dead presidents, rolled them into five-hundred dollar bank rolls, tangled rubber bands around them and dropped them in the duffle bags sitting on the floor. When she finished counting the loot, she did the math on how much she made and how much more she owed Bartise. After she looked at the figures she came up with, she sighed and laid back in her chair. Although she was giving Bartise payments consistently, it felt like she'd never be out of debt with him.

The crazy part about it was the debt she owed wasn't even hers to have to settle. It was actually her father, Jock's bill. He acquired it when he hijacked Bartise's cocaine and skipped town. By the time the kingpin's hittaz pinpointed Chrissy's old man's location, the son of a bitch was gone and so was their boss's drugs. Bartise, not being a man to take a loss, was going to see to it that someone paid for Jock's sins. He found that perfect person the moment he laid eyes on his daughter.

Chrissy was young and stunningly beautiful. On top of that she hadn't been touched and that made her

11

a hot commodity. Bartise took it upon himself to take Chrissy as a form of payment, adding her to his already growing list of concubines. It took some time to break her in and get her to follow his rules and regulations. But in the end little mama proved to be a nice addition to his collection. She was submissive, fit, feminine and friendly. Out of all his girls Chrissy was hands down Bartise's favorite, and all the other women knew it. He showered them all with cash, gifts, shopping sprees and cars of their choosing. But when it came to Chrissy, she got a few extra things just so she'd know she was special.

Chrissy thought being one of Bartise's girls wasn't that bad until bitchez started coming up missing. It fucked with her mental that the girls thought it wasn't a big deal when the others had gone M.I.A. Nijah, one of the sister wives she'd grown close to, told her it was best she minded her business and stayed in her place. Chrissy's curiosity got the best of her though. She went snooping for the reason behind the women vanishing. Once Bartise caught wind of Chrissy's private investigative work, he called her into his study for a special viewing. He showed her footage of the missing women she'd been asking about. She cried silently when she saw Bartise's thugs torture and kill them without remorse. She was told this happened to all of the women who attempted to leave Bartise without giving him the proper compensation.

CHAPTER TWO

Chrissy sat before Bartise's desk as he smoked a vape pen. She had glassy pink eyes and her cheeks were drenched. Snot slid out of her left nostril. She snorted it back up and wiped her nose with her fist. Bartise blew out a cloud and passed her his handkerchief. She blew her nose and wiped it.

"May I—may I ask you something?" Chrissy asked timidly, fearful of his reaction. She kept her hand near the left sleeve of her blouse where she'd hidden a gold steak knife she'd stolen from the kitchen on the way to his study. She was fully prepared to give him one hell of a fight if he felt like raising a hand to her for what she was about to ask.

Bartise nodded and then sucked on the end of his vape pen. "If I—if I decided I wanted to leave? What would—what would be the proper compensation?"

Bartise stopped smoking the vape pen and took a breath. He massaged his chin as he looked at the floor and thought over what he'd been asked. He took a few more pulls from his vape pen before giving his answer. "You know Christina, you've become someone very near and dear to my heart. In fact, I'd go so far as to say you're my favorite outta all of my wives. Still, I'm not gonna make you stay here if you don't want to be here. I'm also not gonna allow you to fly the coop without kicking a lil' cash back up to me either. So, let's just say if I were to let chu walk outta here right now? Do you think $500,000 would be too much to ask for?" Chrissy shook her head as a fresh set of tears spilled down her cheeks. She wiped them away and sniffled like she had the flu.

13

"Good. Fuckin' great 'cause that's the cost for your freedom."

"What do you suggest I do to get you your money?"

"Beats the hell outta me. Whatever you gotta, I guess," Bartise replied. "You can shake ya lil' ass, suck, fuck or work part time at iHop for all I care. It makes no difference to me as long as I get what I'm due." He went back to sucking on the vape pen. Chrissy nodded and wiped her wet cheeks with the handkerchief.

"May I be excused?"

Bartise nodded and blew a cloud up at the ceiling. Chrissy got up and walked to the door. She was about to walk through it when Bartise called her back. She turned around to him with a raised eyebrow. "Do me a favor and return that steak knife to the proper kitchen drawer, please. It's 24k solid gold. It ran yours truly a pretty lil' penny." Chrissy's face scrunched with confusion wondering how he knew she concealed a steak knife in her sleeve. "You never know when you're being watched, shorty, or listened to for that matter. I have eyes and ears everywhere."

Chrissy didn't say a word as she walked out of the study, leaving Bartise with his thoughts and vape pen.

Chrissy got to work to pay off her father's debt asap. She stripped at Big Daddy's and a couple of other clubs. She also did OnlyFans and worked as an escort on the side. She ran into Jayvon in Big Daddy's by chance and they hit it off rather quickly. Once they started talking it was like they'd known each other forever. Every night that she stood outside waiting for her ride, Jayvon would find some excuse to come across the street to holler at her. They'd laugh and talk until Purp came to pick her up.

Once Chrissy felt comfortable enough with Jayvon she told him about her situation. He learned that in addition to being a stripper that she was an escort to some very sophisticated business men. They paid her nicely and they tipped well. It didn't matter to Jayvon what she did for a living or what she was doing it for. His gut instinct told him she was more than her occupation. There were layers to her, and he was going to peel every last one of them back until he knew all of her.

Chrissy and Jayvon became a couple while she was still being held prisoner in Bartise's mansion. Jayvon vowed to help her raise the loot she needed to pay Bartise for her release. Ever since then her, Jayvon and Chyna had been doing everything they could to run it up and see to it that Chrissy was a free woman one day soon.

Chrissy heard someone knocking at the door and got up from her chair. She took a quick look through the peephole to see who was at the door. She unlocked the door and allowed Jayvon inside. She turned around to him after locking the door, kissing him on the lips and taking a seat back at the table.

"So, what are we looking like, baby?" Chrissy asked.

"We came off a'ight, shorty," Jayvon replied, pulling a wrinkled brown paper bag out of the front of his jeans and dumping it on the table top. He sat at the table counterclockwise from Chrissy and pulled three mini bottles of Russian Vodka out of his pocket. He sat all three of them in front of Chrissy. She didn't waste any time cracking them open and guzzling them down. "Damn, ma, take it easy. Them shits ain't goin' nowhere."

Chrissy took the zig zag rolling papers from out of her handbag along with a small baggie of Cali Kush. She went about the task of rolling a blunt while Jayvon studied her. Although Chrissy was still as beautiful as she was the first day he laid eyes on her, she was beginning to show signs of aging. He chalked it up to all of the stress they were under trying to run up a check to pay that nigga Bartise off. Not only was she smoking like an Indian chief, she was drinking like a sailor and popping Percocets like they were breath mints.

Jayvon knew that Chrissy was shaken by Bartise. It made him feel less than a man knowing his lady didn't think he could protect her. This pissed him off to no end, and thoughts of murder impregnated his mind. He didn't have a stick but he knew where he could get one. Augustus, the old man he worked for, kept a rather large gun collection. He showed it to him and Chyna when he invited them to his house for a Christmas party last year. On top of that, the old nigga stayed strapped during business hours at the restaurant. He was pretty sure Augustus would give him a piece if he were to ask. Hell, he'd probably go along with him on the mission.

Javon got the thought in his head to give Bartise and his lapdogs, Purp and Stutter-Box the business. Then he, Chyna and Chrissy would take the money they had and leave New York in their rearview.

16

"Yeah. That's what it is. Soon as I see son's ugly-ass face I'ma give 'em the business and we gon' get the fuck up outta here."

"Bae, what're you talking about?" Chrissy looked at him strangely while sitting at the table with two handfuls of money.

"I'm talkin' about puttin' ya man Bartise inna bag, takin' that loot, grabbin' lil' bro and fleeing the city."

Chrissy took a deep breath and sat the money on the table top. This wasn't the first time Jayvon had brought up wasting Bartise. "Babe, you can't do that!"

Jayvon became angrier. "And why in the fuck not? I'm not afraid of that nigga. And I'm damn sho' not afraid of Purp or Stutter-Box, with his non talkin' ass . All I gotta do is get close enough to guarantee I won't miss and blow homeboy off the map. But I'd have to get rid of Purp and Stutter-Box right after 'cause once I take out the top dawg, I know they're gonna be fiending for a taste of my blood."

This shit can actually work if a nigga plan it right. All I gotta do now is get a piece from OG.

Chrissy got on her knees in front of Jayvon and held him at his waist. She looked up into his eyes with the saddest look he'd ever seen in his life. The look she gave him made him want to kiss her, hold her and tell her over and over again that everything was going to be alright. Staring down at her, Jayvon swept the hair out of her face and caressed her cheek.

Chrissy's eyes pooled with tears and threatened to slide down her cheeks. "Baby, I'm on my knees, and I'm begging you not to kill him."

17

"Everytime I talk about gettin' rid of this nigga, you talk me outta it, yo. I'm getting tired of that shit," Jayvon confessed.

"Jayvon, Bartise is dangerous." The moment Chrissy said this she cussed herself out in her head. She knew men had egos and she'd probably bruised his ego by stating the obvious.

"Dangerous? Dangerous? I'm dangerous, sweetheart." Jayvon frowned, smacking his hand against his chest.

"Baby, if you knock Bartise out the way we'll have hella steppas after us. We'll be on the run for the rest of our lives."

Jayvon pulled Chrissy up to her feet so they'd be at eye level before he said what was next on his mind. "You're my Doll. My word is bond. I'll go to war with Satan and all of Hell behind you." He kissed her and wrapped both his arms around her. Chrissy never felt more safe than she did when she was in the comfort of Jayvon's embrace. She closed her eyes for a moment and exhaled.

"I love you, Von."

"I love you, too."

"How much?"

"More than you'll ever know."

Chrissy looked up at him with teary eyes. "Then promise me you'll stick to our plan."

Jayvon wiped the wetness from Chrissy's eyes as he stared in her face. His seeing her so vulnerable softened his heart and made him melt like butter in her hands. He took a breath and nodded. A smile instantly formed across her lips. She hugged and kissed him like he'd proposed.

"Thank you, Von. This is the best way to go about things. You'll see," Chrissy assured him.

"Now let's finish countin' up this bread. I told the old man I was goin' on my thirty-minute lunch break and that was an hour ago."

"Okay. But first, gemme some lip, Big Daddy," Chrissy closed her eyes and puckered up. Jayvon grinned and kissed her. He tried to pull away but she held fast, kissing deeper and longer. "Damn, baby, I see yo' pet python is awake." She grabbed his package and he grunted. She leaned so close she could smell the buffalo wings he consumed earlier at the strip club that night.

"Yep. It's feedin' time."

"Oh, yeah? Well, what does he eat?" Chrissy asked softly, licking her top lip and massaging his package.

"Fine ass stripper bitchez from Harlem."

Chrissy laughed and kissed him. Shit got hot and heavy between them, real quick. Before they knew it, they were down to their underwear and Jayvon was scooping her up in his arms.

"Wait a minute, handsome, are you forgetting about work?"

"Don't trip. I'll make it a quickie."

Jayvon continued to make out with Chrissy as he carried her over to the bed. He laid her down and gave her a serious piping.

CHAPTER THREE

Chyna's forehead shone from perspiration as he fled from danger. He occasionally glanced over his shoulder to see if the threats to his life were still on his heels. He was hot, sweaty and tired as shit, but he knew the moment he stopped running he was a dead man. Chyna had two Puerto Rican shooters after him. Murder was on their minds and Tec-9s were in their gloved hands. Their boss was thirsty for blood but not just anyone's blood—Chyna's blood!

Chyna had convinced Draco, a dopeman from Spanish Harlem to give him a G-pack to hustle for some dough. For every package the young nigga moved he'd get a hundred dollars, the rest would get kicked back up to Draco. Chyna was able to get the work off with no problem, but he didn't give the head honcho his cut. Instead, he used the money to buy groceries, pay some past due bills and pitch in for his brother to get his girlfriend, Chrissy back from this notorious drug dealer.

"You can run but chu can't hide, pendejo!" One of the Puerto Ricans shouted at Chyna's back. He was the shortest of the two and coincidentally his nickname was Shorty.

"Pinche moreno, you're gonna pay for stealing from mi familia," the other Puerto Rican, Jorge, shouted. The men slowed up running and cocked their Tec-9s. They upped their weapons and opened fire at Chyna. Chyna clenched his jaws, ducking low and zig zagging. Bullets deflected off lamp posts, stop signs and nearby buildings. Unfortunately, a man coming out of a bodega with a gyro and a Coca

Cola walked right into the line of fire. His bottle of Coke exploded, and his sandwich was shredded as they were pelted by bullets. He collapsed on the sidewalk with his blood dripping into the gutter. All the gunfire caused hysteria. Pedestrians ran back and forth across the street to avoid catching any stray bullets.

"Fuck! This fuckin' cuete jammed!" Jorge complained trying to dislodge the bullet that rendered his Tec-9 useless.

"I told you we shoulda brought the revolvers instead," Shorty told him after firing the last of his ammo. He ejected its magazine, pulled another one from the small of his back, and loaded it into his Tec-9.

Once Jorge had released the bullet that jammed his stick, he and Shorty went back to chasing Chyna. Chyna, still running, glanced back and forth over his shoulder. He ran out into the crosswalk and neglected to look in front of him.

Boonk!

Chyna flipped over the hood of a speeding Dodge Challenger and landed on his side, wincing. The driver feared he'd killed him and drove away in a hurry. Wicked smiles spread across the Puerto Rican shooters' lips seeing Chyna at their mercy.

"Yeah, we've got cho black ass now," Jorge licked his top row of teeth as he and Shorty stepped off the curb. Chyna's heart thudded madly watching them lift their Tecs to finish him off. He could have made a run for it, but he was sure they'd gun him down before he could escape. Still, Chyna wasn't one to go down without a fight. He was raised to keep fighting until his dying breath and that's exactly what he was going to do.

Chyna slipped his barber razor from out of his right back pocket and flicked it open. The sun reflected off its blade, causing it to gleam.

Jorge shook his head and laughed. He looked at Shorty and said, "Look, this dumb ass lil' nigga, brought a knife to a gunfight."

Urrrrrk! Boom! Da-doom-doom!

A glossy purple Mercedes-Benz G-Wagon slammed into Jorge, driving over him, making his bones crack and pop. Shorty was stunned at first but once his brain registered what had occurred, he went to open fire. He stopped cold in his tracks when the passenger hopped out the front seat with what looked like a space-age weapon. It was big, long, black and came equipped with a scope, infrared laser and suppressor. The man behind the trigger was more intimidating than his assault rifle. All Shorty could see were a pair of menacing red eyes peeking over the purple bandana tied around the lower half of his face. The brazen man was of a slim, muscular build and his hair was styled in reddish-brown dreadlocks.

"Drop dee gun batty bowi, or me swear me a knock da candy outta ya pinata!" The man behind the bandana spoke aggressively. His Jamaican accent was so thick there wasn't any doubt he was born on the island.

Seeing the shotta had the drop on him, Shorty knew it would be wise to give up, so he tossed his Tec aside and lifted his hands. At this time, still holding the barber's razor, Chyna slowly rose to his feet with pain written on his face.

"You good, king?" Dolph, the driver, asked Chyna from behind the wheel. He was a tall, clean shaven, dark-skinned brother with a bald head that shined like a polished bowling ball. He wore gold wire frame Cartier glasses, diamond earrings, and two round cut tennis necklaces; one longer than the other.

Chyna nodded with a pained look on his face, saying, "Y—yeah—I'll be okay." He then closed his barber's razor and slid it into his back pocket.

"You niggaz know who we work for?" Shorty mad dogged Bocka.

"Yeah, we know, bowi, we don't give a fuck, either." Bocka held his mad dog stare.

"Hop in, king, but watch yo' sneaks on my leather seats," Dolph told Chyna, motioning him over with a jeweled hand. "The God just got this bitch detailed, nah mean?"

"I got chu, bruh," Chyna said, holding his aching side. He opened the back door of the G-Wagon and climbed into the backseat.

"Bawse man, give Bocka da word and me a swiss cheese dis piece of shit!" Bocka spoke to Dolph but kept his eyes on Shorty.

At this time police car sirens were blaring in the distance as they were speeding to this very location.

"Nah, we gon' let homie live, Bocka. Today's a beautiful day," Dolph smiled while taking in his surroundings. "The sun is out; the birds are chirpin' and fine ass women are out by the dozens. I wouldn't wanna ruin the day by givin' you the okay to air-out my Mexican brethren here."

"I'm Puerto Rican, asshole," Shorty sneered and clenched his jaws. He hated to be called anything other than what he was and usually brought violence to anyone who did.

"Yeah, whatever, muthafucka, a spic's a spic in my book." Dolph let him know. He tilted his Cartier glasses so Shorty could get a good look at him. The milky white eye was disturbing to him and brought an icy chill down his back. "Run along now, Shorty and be sure to tell that nigga Draco that the young king is under the K.O.T now. So should any harm come to him, me and mine will lay waste to his entire lot. Ya dig?" He smiled, showcasing all thirty-two of his perfectly white teeth. He then scowled and told Bocka to let Shorty go.

Bocka lowered his assault rifle at his side and threw his head to the right, "Get da fuck outta here before me change me mind!"

Shorty kept his eyes on Bocka as he slowly turned around. He had the feeling that he was going to get shot down as soon as he turned to run. He walked away and then took off in a full sprint.

Bocka hopped back into the front passenger seat, slammed the door shut and Dolph sped away.

CHAPTER FOUR

Dolph sped up the street nodding his head to the blaring music and taking in his surroundings. He glanced up at the rearview mirror and saw Chyna staring out of the back window. Chyna was a handsome, mahogany complexion, sixteen-year-old with curly hair that reached his shoulders. The bumps and bruises he wore were evidence of the hard knock life he led. He had more scars on him than he cared to count, but the most noticeable ones were the three keloid scars overlapping each other on his right arm. He'd earned them when he was caught stealing a lobster from a fish market in Manhattan. The owner, a Chinese man, attacked him with a meat cleaver, with every intention of beheading him. Luckily for Chyna, a few brothers saw what was happening and intervened. They beat the brakes off the irate Chinese man and dumped his meat cleaver in the storm drain while Chyna made a fast getaway.

Chyna managed to escape with one measly lobster but that was all he needed. It was Jayvon's seventeenth birthday and he wanted to make him something special. He'd overheard him say he'd never had lobster before so he wanted to surprise him. He had already stolen a pack of T-bone steaks, garlic bread, a box of instant mashed potatoes, and a bottle of Moët & Chandon from the corner bodega. So the birthday dinner he had in mind for his brother would be complete.

When Chyna made it back home, he cleaned his wounds as best as he could and patched them up. He went on to cook his brother's birthday meal so he'd have it by the time he came home from work. He'd gotten halfway done with cooking when he suddenly felt lightheaded and passed out from loss of blood. When he finally came to, he was in the hospital with Jayvon caressing his forehead. Chyna had been given liquids and a blood transfusion to replace the plasma he'd lost. He and his brother spent the rest of their night together talking and laughing. They eventually fell asleep with Jayvon lying in his hospital bed at one end and Chyna at the other.

Dolph noticed Chyna wince while rubbing his side. He turned the volume of the music down and addressed him. "Yo, king, you a'ight back there? You needa go to the 'spital or somethin'?"

"Nah, I'm good, son." Chyna smiled weakly.

"I hear you, king, you tryna thug that shit out. Respect," Dolph said, throwing up his fist. "But on some real shit, if you really feel like you needa go, holla at the god, I gotchu faded."

Chyna nodded. "No doubt."

Dolph shook up with Chyna from over his shoulder. It was an exclusive handshake every member of the King of Thieves performed upon greeting and departing from each other. They normally didn't do it with prospects until they were made official but everyone had mad love for Chyna. He had all the qualities of a stalwart soldier and they definitely wanted him a part of their organization. Still, there weren't any walk-ons in their thing. Everyone wearing that K.O.T ink had to be initiated. Niggas had to know what the fuck you were made of. They couldn't have just anyone bearing their mark.

Bocka lit up a fat ass Rastafarian blunt, hit it a few times, and passed it to Dolph. After Dolph indulged, he glanced up at the rearview mirror at Chyna, extending the blunt over his shoulder toward him. "You tryna hit this shit?"

Chyna stared at the blunt pinched between Dolph's fingers like it was a poisonous rattlesnake. He'd never gotten high before and his brother had always told him to never smoke with anyone who already had a blunt rolled. The blunt could be laced with something that could give him a serious mind-fuck.

Despite his brother's warning, Chyna decided to go ahead and take a few tokes. He'd done his fair share of miscellaneous shit to get in favor of the Kings and didn't want to do anything to fuck up his good standing with them. Taking a deep breath, Chyna took the blunt from Dolph and took a drag. The smoke hit his lungs like a sniper's bullet and sent him into a coughing fit. Dolph and Bocka exchanged glances while laughing.

"Goddamn, yo, my—my muthafuckin' chest hurt," Chyna complained, smacking his chest as he passed the blunt back to Dolph.

"Lil' homie got them virgin lungs. I guess we popped my young nigga's cherry, huh?" Dolph told Bocka before shaking up with him.

"Youth, you good back dere?" Bocka asked Chyna, turning halfway around in his seat.

"Yeah, I'll be a'ight, bro," Chyna replied, smacking his chest and looking at the K.O.T tatted on Bocka's arm. He'd had it for so long it was beginning to fade. K.O.T also known as Kings of

Thieves, had an infamous reputation that stretched throughout the five boroughs of New York. Their name was synonymous with taking niggaz bitches, money, drugs, jewelry, whips, and even their lives—if the price was right. They flew the colors purple and yellow. Purple stood for royalty while yellow stood for gold. They all rocked the same ink K.O.T, with a gemmed crown sitting cocked on the letter 'K'.

"Yo, Dolph, when you gon' put me down, B? I'm tired of being broke. I'm tryna get money with y'all niggaz," Chyna said, licking his lips and rubbing his hands together greedily. The Kings of Thieves were known for getting money, so he was definitely with any schemes they had.

Dolph was about to answer Chyna when he was interrupted by the ringing of one of his two iPhones. The black one was his personal cellular phone and the silver one was the business cellphone. They were both lying up front beside him.

"Hold on, God. That's the money callin'," Dolph told him before answering the silver cellphone. "Yeah, who's on the menu? You know me and the Kings are always ready to eat. Wait, wait, wait, wait, I'm driving. I'ma give my son the jack so he can write down this info. Hold on." He passed Bocka the cellphone. "Grab that ink pen outta the glove box and write down the info for me, King," he told Bocka and he did as he was instructed. He disconnected the call then showed Dolph the job they were supposed to do and how much they were going to see off the lick. Dolph responded by licking his top row of teeth and sucking them. A smile spread across his lips displaying his perfectly white teeth again.

"Yo, youngin', I've got good news," Dolph announced, glancing up at the rearview mirror at Chyna. Chyna threw his head back like *What's up?* "Today is the day you get your officials."

"Hell yeah. I'm tryna get to this schmoney," Chyna replied, rubbing his hands together again.

"Say, youth, yew gettin' down," Bocka grinned, shaking up with Chyna.

Dolph cranked the volume back up on his stereo's system and zipped through traffic. He mashed the gas pedal and the G-Wagon flew up the street.

CHAPTER FIVE

Draco and his goons crowded around his bunk watching an underground fight on his cellphone. Their eyes were fixated on the match, and it was so entertaining they didn't want to miss a second of it.

"Hamza beatin' the brakes off this kid!" DeMozzio told his right-hand man, Draco. He was a twenty-four-year-old Puerto Rican kid who wore his hair in a tapered fade. At five-foot-eight, he weighed a measly 140-pounds, but for what he lacked in size, he made up for with courage.

"He better. I've got fifty bucks riding on this nigga!" Draco smiled at the screen of his iPhone. At twenty-five-years-old, he stood six-feet-tall and had muscles that threatened to split the seams of his prison uniform. He rocked Pop Smoke braids and a goatee. Draco was a man as dangerous as the weapon he was named after. Most didn't dare to challenge him and his cutthroat Boricuas. While the police ruled the day in Spanish Harlem, Draco and his brethren ruled the night. They made their fortune pumping drugs in the slums but that eventually came to an end, thanks to Draco's baby mama, Sabina . Little mama was the reason why he was incarcerated now.

Having had enough of his infidelity, she decided to get her lick back. Shorty didn't fuck someone else to get even though, instead, she hit all of his stash spots and skipped town. Draco was broke but he managed to scrape up the bread for a private investigator. Although it cost a pretty penny to hire the former NYPD detective, he was worth every dollar. He managed to track down Sabina and some new nigga she was playing house with. Draco was going to send his hittaz to do the job but his son's mother stealing his bread was personal. He decided to handle the situation by himself but DeMozzio, being the loyalist he was, insisted on riding with him.

Word traveled at the speed of a bullet in the hood, so it wasn't long before Sabina got word Draco was out for her blood. She honestly wasn't worried about him catching up with her since she moved so far out in the sticks, but her boo knew better than she did. He was well aware of Draco's reputation. He knew he wasn't the kind of man that you'd want after you so he pushed the issue of getting out of dodge.

***

Antoine darted to the front door with luggage and designer travel bags filled with Draco's money. He snatched the door open. He was about to run outside when he noticed his girl wasn't on his heels.

"What the fuck this bitch doin'?" Antoine said under his breath. He then shouted over his shoulder. "Girl, brang yo' ass on. I'm not tryna run into yo' crazy ass baby daddy!"

"Nigga, I'm comin'. I'm tryna pack the rest of these clothes!" Sabina shouted from the bedroom.

"With all the loot we got, you can just buy all that shit over again."

"Boy, please, no tellin' where we'll end up. I may not ever find this shit again!"

"Fuck this, I'm gone!" Antoine fled the house, leaving the front door open.

"How the hell you gon' leave me behind and take the money I stole, nigga? You got me fucked up!" Sabina ran out of the bedroom with luggage and her nine-month old son strapped to her back. She stepped onto the front porch, sitting one of her suitcases down, and pulling the front door shut behind her.

She ran as fast as her stilettos would allow her across the lawn. She saw Antoine standing at the open hatch of the Tahoe she'd purchased a couple of days ago. He was holding his gun at his side and keeping a close eye on the block.

"Yo, shorty, hurry the fuck up. A primered van with tints as black as my ass just crept up the block. Ain't no tellin' who that might be," Antoine told her as he took one of the suitcases from her and placed it inside the back of the Tahoe.

"Bae, yo' ass is too fuckin' paranoid. That nigga ain't found us that quick," Sabina told him. "We move too frequently, you needa just chill out." She lovingly caressed the side of his face as she stared into his eyes.

Antoine closed his eyes briefly and took a deep breath. "Maybe you're right. Maybe I am just a lil' paranoid, but I'ma street nigga, baby. My paranoia has kept me alive so for so l—"

Antoine's eyes bubbled as confusion set on his face. His chest exploded in a crimson mass splattering against Sabina's face. Antoine, still holding his gun, fell in the driveway twitching. Sabina was so choked up she couldn't scream. She looked up the driveway where the bullets came from. An infrared laser beam shone from the darkness as someone walked toward her. A man wearing all *black and a transparent plastic mask emerged. He had an assault rifle with a muzzle on it. The 100-round drum that it was equipped with looked like an oversized hockey puck.*

"Manny!" Sabina gasped as she recited Draco's government name. She dove to the ground as bullets zipped in her direction. The side view mirror exploded and the windshield shattered. Instantly, the Tahoe's alarm blared crazily. Then Sabina's baby started wailing. She scrambled upon her feet and ran out of the yard. She sobbed and screamed for help, looking over her shoulder to see how close Draco was on her heels. "Help me! Somebody help me! Oh, my God, please! Somebody help!" She yelled as she looked around, seeing the lights of nearby houses pop on.

Draco stopped chasing after Sabina . He lifted his assault rifle and focused its laser at her back. He was about to lay her down until he realized he'd be murdering his son in the process.

"Fuck," Draco said under his breath. He was about to lower his assault rifle until another idea popped inside of his head. He leveled his weapon at the back of Sabina 's knees and blew them out from under her. She collided with the sidewalk with her face twisted in agony.

The van that Antoine spotted earlier pulled up behind Draco. He looked over his shoulder at his homeboy, DeMozzio. He was wearing the same transparent mask and duds as him.

"I got this bitch, You get the loot out the hatch of that truck!" Draco told him. Cradling his assault

rifle, he ran in Sabina 's direction while DeMozzio went to carry out his orders.

When Draco walked upon Sabina, she was sobbing and trying to crawl away. Her son was crying and wailing even louder. Seeing his son in such a way softened Draco's heart. He transformed from a coldblooded killa to a concerned father. He pressed his black Air Force one against Sabina 's back, drew a small knife from his back pocket and sliced his son free of bondage.

"Shhhhh. Shhhhh. It's me, papi, it's daddy. See?" Draco lifted his transparent mask so his baby boy could see his face. The infant quieted down when recognition set in. Draco kissed his son on his chubby cheek and pulled his mask back down over his face. At this time, the police cars sirens were blaring as law enforcement was approaching. That nigga Draco didn't give a fuck though. He came out there to do a job and he wasn't leaving until it was done.

CHAPTER SIX

"Yo, I loaded the money inside the van, let's get the fuck outta here," DeMozzio told Draco. He'd just screeched to a stop in the middle of the residential street.

"Yo, son, take my prince," Draco passed his heir to DeMozzio through the driver's window. When he took the boy, he started whimpering for his father. He comforted him before stepping to his business. "It's a'ight, papi. Daddy will be right back, I promise." He kissed two of his fingers and placed them on the baby's lips.

DeMozzio bounced the baby up and down on his knee, trying to get him to stop crying. He focused his attention out of the window as he watched his father, Draco, reveal his identity to Sabina and riddle her upper body with bullets. Draco cradled his assault rifle with both hands as he retreated back to the van. As soon as he hopped in, he tossed his weapon into the back of the van and took his crying baby in his hands.

"Let's get the fuck outta here," Draco said, lifting up his transparent mask. DeMozzio nodded, threw the van in drive and floored that bitch. The van zipped up the block but DeMozzio slammed on the brakes. Two police cars came to a squealing halt in front of him. He put the van in reverse, threw his arm over the passenger seat and looked over his shoulder out of the back window. He floored the gas pedal again and the van zipped backwards down the street. Again, DeMozzio slammed on the brakes as two more police cars squealed to a halt behind him.

35

"Fuck it, papi. You and I always said we'd hold court in the streets before we go back to the clinka," DeMozzio said, throwing the van in park and grabbing his machine gun. After making sure his stick was locked and loaded, he reached in the back of the van and grabbed Draco's assault rifle. *"I'm ready when you are, bro."*

Draco looked through the windshield, to see the police using their whips as shields while pointing their guns at them. He looked out of the back window and the second set of policemen were doing the same thing. He could hear one of them barking orders out of a megaphone but he didn't pay him any mind.

Draco looked at his assault rifle and then down at his baby boy. The little guy had somehow fallen asleep through all the chaos. DeMozzio looked at his godson and saw how peaceful he looked in his father's arms. He glanced up at Draco's face and saw the dilemma in his eyes. It was then he knew he couldn't allow his friend to follow through with the pact he made and put his only son in jeopardy. Though Draco may not be able to raise the boy on the outside, he could watch him grow up and give him guidance while on the inside.

"It's okay, poppa, some pacts are made to be broken," DeMozzio placed a reassuring hand on Draco's shoulder.

Draco lifted his transparent mask above his head and looked him in the eyes. *"Gracias, hermano."*

"Don't mention it, hermano. Familia," DeMozzio shook up with Draco and then he kissed his godson on the forehead.

"Familia," Draco replied, shaking up with him.

"Okay. We're gonna give up!" DeMozzio yelled out of the window, pulling off his transparent mask and tossing it outside. He threw his assault rifle out next and outstretched his gloved hand to Draco. "Gemme your cuete."

Draco gave him his stick and he threw it out of the driver's window. DeMozzi then followed the policemen's orders to remove the key out of the ignition and toss them out of the window. He was then ordered to open the driver's door and step out with his hands up. DeMozzio threw open the driver's door. He was about to step out when he felt Draco grab his shoulder. When he looked at him he saw a seriousness in his eyes he'd never seen in all his years of knowing him.

"It looks like this one may lead to us spending the rest of our lives inside. But I want chu to know that this thing that you did for me, letting me break our pact on the account of my prince, won't be overlooked," Draco assured him. "I swear on the life of my only child, we're gonna live like kings whether we're out here or in there. I give you my word as a man. As your brother. As your best friend."

DeMozzio nodded before stepping out of the van with his hands up. Draco placed a tender kiss on his son's forehead before laying him down in the back of the van. He then threw open the passenger door, held his hands up, and stepped out into the street.

***

Hamza threw the final blow that sealed his victory. As soon as his opponent crashed to the ground, a call from "Shorty" came through. Draco had been looking forward to this call and he didn't want anyone listening to what he was being told.

"A'ight, y'all niggaz gotta bounce. I've gotta take this call." Draco stood up and waved everyone out of his cell. They came together and walked out like a classroom of kids headed for lunch. The only one that hung back was DeMozzio. He posted up outside the cell and folded his arms across his chest. He played lookout while Draco discussed whatever business he had with Shorty over the phone.

"What up, Shorty?" Draco answered the call. He paced the floor listening to what he was being told. DeMozzi could tell by the look on his face he'd gotten some bad news. "Okay. You weren't able to get that bread, but please tell me you were able to leave that dog-ass nigga lyin' belly up."

"Sorry, Draco, but he got away." Shorty admitted.

"Fuck! Fuck! Fuck!" Draco cussed and swung his fist wildly.

"Hermano, keep it down, you're drawin' attention," DeMozzi told him in a hushed tone. A few inmates had looked up at their cell.

Draco ran his hand down his face. He took a moment to get his mind right before talking back to the caller. "Nah. Don't worry about it. You did the best you could. Sorry about Jorge." He disconnected the call. "That's what I get for sending a couple of fuckin' amateurs to do the jobs of pinche professionals."

"What's going on?" DeMozzio questioned with concern.

Draco propped his arm against the top bunk. He motioned DeMozzio over and told him about his cousins fuck up.

"It will be okay, bro. Gettin' that lil' bitta money woulda probably made us lazy anyway," DeMozzio said, giving him a brotherly hug. "In the meantime, we'll have to keep applying pressure to these weak muthafuckaz to guarantee we eat."

Draco felt like he didn't deserve to have a friend as loyal as DeMozzio. It was all his fault that they were doing forever and a day. It was out of love that DeMozzio insisted on rolling out with him to drop his baby mama and her new nigga. They didn't have a dollar between them since their incarceration which was why they started extorting mothafuckaz for the items they needed. Draco tried reaching out to the streets to collect the bread from the hustlers that owed him but they all changed their numbers and dropped off the face of the earth. Chyna was the only person he could think of that was free and still indebted to him. The young nigga only owed him a stack, but Draco was broke as a joke and as desperate as a two-dollar whore. He needed that stack like a flat booty bitch needed a BBL and that's why he sent his people to collect on his behalf.

"You're right, bro, we're on these niggaz heads. Come on. Let's go see what the clan is up to," Draco replied, nudging DeMozzio as he walked out of their cell.

CHAPTER SEVEN

Dolph stashed his Mercedes-Benz G-Wagon at a safe location. Bocka,Chyna and him got suited, booted, masked and armed for the mission he'd taken on their behalf. Dolph rolled out a map and used Hot Wheels toy cars to show his crew how they'd perform the hit. Once he was sure everyone knew their roles, he rolled up the map like it was an ancient scroll and set it on fire. He waited until the flames had devoured half of the map before tossing it aside. Everyone piled inside of the van they'd use for that day's assignment and left the disclosed location. The map lay half a mile away burning and curling into soot.

***

Jerry came out the back of the Chinese restaurant sniffing and pulling on his nose. He was chaperoned by two Japanese men in black suits and leather dress shoes. One wore round-lens glasses and a diamond piercing below his bottom lip. He had a shiny baldhead with fire breathing dragons and Japanese letters inked on it. The second one wore his hair in dreadlocks which had been pulled up into a bun. He also sported diamond earrings and three diamond studded necklaces, all differing in size and length, around his neck.

Jerry Stevens was a five-foot-eleven white dude of a slender build. He had shoulder length blonde hair and a face as bald as a newborn baby's ass. His eyes were glassy and his left nostril was leaking. He'd copped his supply from this particular dealer before so he knew he had some fire on his hands. He was past due for a taste so he fed his demon before making his departure from the establishment. The powder was so potent it hit him like the disciplining hand of a Mississippi pimp.

Old Jerry was a superstar attorney who had it all: money, cars, women, anything he could dream of. There was no disputing the fact he thought of himself as a God among men. But that was probably more so due to the large amounts of cocaine he shoved up his nose and how he managed to wiggle his way out of his legal troubles. His connections and a few well placed dollars may have gotten him out of a prison bid but the streets had their own justice system he'd have to answer to.

In addition to Jerry's addiction to coke, he had a thing for girls, really young girls—twelve, but no older than fifteen to be exact. This last poor child he'd sunk his hooks into just so happened to be the fourteen-year-old daughter of a very prominent banker namedCalogero Brancato. Though Calogero was legit, he still maintained relationships with old childhood buddies of his who held mob ties. These connected men loved Calogero like white women loved black pro athletes so naturally when he requested their assistance in making Jerry's predatorial ass a memory, they jumped at the opportunity. To keep their hands clean of the act, the mobsters contacted outside sources to get the job done. That's where Dolph and his Kings of Thieves came into play. Once Jerry was murked, the authorities wouldn't be expecting a band of trigger happy black youths from the slums of Brooklyn to be behind the hit. So, the Kings were perfect for the job.

Jerry slid onto the leather seats of the SUV and Corey, the tattooed head Japanese bodyguard, slammed the door shut behind him. While Lowkey, the dreadlock haired bodyguard, was sliding in behind the wheel of the truck, Corey was taking in the scenery to make sure there wasn't anyone or anything around that would be a threat to his employer's safety. After ensuring there wasn't any imminent danger, Corey hopped into the front passenger seat. He picked up the automatic weapon he'd left behind while escorting Jerry inside the restaurant. Lowkey gave another scan of the area before cranking up the truck and pulling out of the parking lot.

"Aye, you guys wanna taste? It's some pretty good stuff," Jerry assured them as he pulled out a rolled up, blue face one hundred dollar bill and a pocket mirror to indulge in his habit.

"No thank you, Mr. Stevens, my partner and I prefer not to be under the influence while working. Your safety is of the utmost importance to us," Corey told him. He took his job very seriously and didn't want to fuck up his track record. He'd been in his line of work for seventeen years, and never has a client of his been killed or injured. He took pride in this.

Jerry nodded understandingly. He realized Corey was absolutely right about being sober while protecting him. They would have trouble holding him down if they were coked-up. Hell, it was bad enough he was burying his face in mountains of cocaine.

Urrrrrrrk!

"What the fuck?" Lowkey's eyes bulged.

"This dick-head must be drunk!" Corey said annoyed.

A banged up Astro van swung out in front of the H2 Hummer, making it screech to a halt. The door of the van slid open! Two men jumped out wearing purple ski masks and bulletproof-vests over their clothes. They upped their tavor assault rifles and moved in on the Hummer. They mad dogged the bodyguards daring them to make a move.

"Oh, shit!" Jerry leaned up front, wiping the cocaine residue from his nose. Seeing the masked gunmen sobered him up quickly. "What the hell are you waiting for dumb-dumb," he said as he smacked the back of Lowkey's head, "Mow these cocksuckas down!"

Lowkey went to run down the masked men and that's when the fireworks started. *Ping, ting, bing, zing!* Sparks flew off the exterior of the bulletproof Hummer as it sped towards the masked gunmen. The masked gunmen dove out of the path of the speeding vehicle and rolled on the ground like they were on fire. They looked up from where they were, then at each other, holding up a thumb. Their gunning at the Hummer was a distraction so Chyna could enact his part in the plan.

"What the hell was that freaky shit back there? Those jack asses were trying to take me out," Jerry said, staring out the back window. He was as high as a satellite a minute ago but that botched hit sobered him up quickly.

43

"No shit, Sherlock!" Lowkey replied, glancing in the side view mirror, to see the masked gunmen running to hop back inside of their getaway car. His brows furrowed when he saw another masked gunman hanging on the side of the Hummer. He looked like he was focussed on activating something out of his sight. "Hey, there's a black kid hanging onto the back of the truck," he told Corey.

Jerry looked out of the back window again and saw exactly who Lowkey was talking about. The masked gunman pressed his middle finger against the window, stooped low, then jumped down to the pavement. He tumbled down the pavement hard and fast. Wincing, he looked up from the ground, to see Corey hanging halfway out of the passenger window. He hoisted up his AR-15 assault rifle and sent bullets zipping at him.

Ping! Ting! Bing! Zink!

Bullets cut into the pavement and debris sprayed up into the air. The masked gunman kept rolling down the street as fast as he could to avoid the line of fire. When he finally stopped he was breathing hard and staring at the back of the Hummer. The Hummer stopped in the middle of the street and sped in reverse toward him. The passenger door was wide open and half of Corey's body was visible. He could see his AR-15 and his leg hanging out of the Hummer. He knew then he had every intention of hopping out of the vehicle and gunning him down.

The masked gunman grabbed hold of the tavor assault rifle he'd dropped when he jumped off the back of the Hummer. He rose to a kneeling position, counting down.

Three...two...one, the masked gunman thought, out of breath. He narrowed his eyes into slits and ducked low.

CHAPTER EIGHT

Ka-boom!

The Hummer burst into flames and hot broken glass. Corey rocketed out of the passenger seat and crashed to the pavement. He rolled around screaming in excruciating agony, desperately to put himself out. Hoisting up his tavor assault rifle, the masked gunman ran towards the burning Hummer, moving like someone who was trained for situations like this. The passenger door of the Hummer swung open and Lowkey hopped out partially ablaze. He screamed horrifically as the fire cooked him like a piece of Popeyes' chicken. The masked gunman and him looked eyes as he ran up on him. Lowkey went to lay him down but he was too slow on the draw. This would prove to be fatal for him because the masked gunman wouldn't show him mercy.

Bullets zipped out of the masked gunman's tavor assault rifle, going right through Lowkey's body, chopping him down. The masked gunman ran up on him continuously firing until he stopped moving. His cheeks ballooned. He threw his gloved hand over his mouth, to keep from throwing up. The smell of burning flesh made him sick to his stomach.

Hearing police car sirens drawing closer to his location, the masked gunman knew he had to act fast. He popped the locks from the door panel and snatched the backdoor open. Jerry's corpse was in the backseat ablaze. The fire had nearly burned his body down to its skeleton. This was a terrifying sight to the masked gunman but he ignored it. He had to get his hands on that merchandise he was toting.

The masked gunman switched hands with his assault rifle when he saw the Louis Vuitton duffle bag beside Jerry. It was partially burning. It was so hot it took him a few tries before he was able grab it out of the backseat. He stomped out the burning duffle bag and peered inside of it. There were six Seran wrapped bricks that hadn't been harmed by the fire. He zipped the duffle bag back up, snatched it up and ran around the back of the Hummer. He stopped dead in his tracks when he saw Corey looking like an Asian Freddy Krueger with smoke billowing from him. Corey mad dogged him and upped his AR-15 to cut him into halves. He had the masked gunman dead to rights and he knew it too.

Boom!

The banged up Astro van slammed into Corey and drove over him. The side of the van slid open and one of the masked gunmen who'd shot up the windshield of the Hummer stuck his head out.

"Come on, nigga!" The masked gunman hollered out to his crime partner, waving him over to hop inside the van. The masked gunman tossed the Louie duffle bag of product inside of the van and hopped in behind it. The masked gunman that slid the door open slid it back closed. The van then took off down the block, growing smaller and smaller until it disappeared.

***

Once the job was done, Dolph and them blew up the Astro van and went to collect their bag for the execution. They headed out to their headquarters where they separated the money among them and the portion they were to kick up to the OG's of their organization. Twenty percent of the profits would go to the three men that made up the Kings of Thieves hierarchy: King Yak, King Shyne and King Morpheus, who was Dolph's older brother. Although the three men were incarcerated for the rest of their lives, they ran the streets from the prisons they were housed in. After Dolph and Bocka got their cut, they would use the rest of their money to pay for attorney fees for their incarcerated members, put money in their commissary, and make sure their families were taken care of.

After divvying up the loot from the initial hit, Dolph went on to divide up the bricks that were inside the Louis Vuitton duffle bag. Chyna loscored. Although he wouldn't see any of the money or blow from the heist, he found satisfaction in knowing he was a part of the team that busted the move that guaranteed his brethren would eat.

"Yo, word to mine, this a nice lil' lick we came up on," Dolph said, leaned back in his chair with a double cup of that Dirty Sprite.

Bocka nodded in agreement, holding smoke hostage in his lungs and then blowing it out. He held a blunt of OG Kush pinched between his fingers and smoke wafted around him like it had taken on a life of its own.

Dolph took a sip from his cups and watched Chyna closely. He loved how he handled himself out there, moving like a professional and all. There was a litter of pups he had to choose from to make a part of the Kings of Thieves. He'd narrowed it down to Chyna and some other kid. They were damn near neck and neck but Chyna wound up making the cut. His competition was great but there was something special about Chyna that led him to being picked. Dolph gave himself until the end of the day to decide who he'd choose to welcome into the ranks. As soon as his mind was made up, he tapped Bocka to call up the other kid and tell him who they were going to go with.

Dolph slid from off his chair, switching hands with his cups and picking up one of the bricks that Chyna managed to salvage from the fire. He walked around the table, sat the brick in front of Chyna, and hung his arm around his shoulders.

"Like I told you before, no one gets a taste of the action their first time out, but since you've proved to be such an asset to the family, I thought I should send you home with a lil' somethin', somethin'. Nah, mean?" Dolph patted Chyna on the shoulder brother-like and took a sip of Dirty Sprite. "Consider that a welcome to the family gift." He nodded to the brick he'd sat in front of him.

Chyna's eyes were as big as bowling balls when he saw the brick. He picked it up and examined it like it was an ancient artifact. He didn't know much about drugs so he couldn't quite estimate the profit he was looking at once he'd gotten it off.

"That bird gotta 'bouta $34,500 dollar price tag in the streets, but I'ma show you how to rock that bitch up," a lazy-eyed Dolph assured him, slurring his speech. That purple syrup had taken its full effect on him and was coursing through his veins. "If we cut it into dimes, you stand to see hella gwap."

All Chyna could think about was how much bread he could make off the bird to put towards Chrissy getting released from Bartise's clutches. Chyna couldn't stop smiling when he pushed away from the table. He shook up with Dolph and then Bocka, patting them both on the back.

"That's love, son. For real, for real. A nigga appreciates this," Chyna said, looking back down at the brick.

"Oh, one more thang, King." Dolph snapped his fingers and motioned Bocka over to them. When Chyna turned around Bocka was walking up to him with something wrapped in a purple bandana. As soon as Bocka unwrapped what was hidden in the fabric, Chyna's eyes doubled in size and the biggest smile spread across his lips. He looked like a kid that unwrapped a toy he always wanted on Christmas morning.

"Go ahead, me youth, me made her me self," Bocka told Chyna proudly. He had his blunt wedged between the fingers of one hand while the other held out the bandana. Chyna picked up the piece lying inside the bandana. He gripped it with both hands, closed one of his eyes and pointed it around the basement. The deadly weapon gleamed. It was a gold-plated .45 semi-automatic with an onyx handle. The pistol was sexy as hell which was why Bocka named it, Naomi. "You like her?"

"Like her? Shiiiit, I think I've fallen in love with this bitch," a grinning Chyna replied jovially.

"Good. 'Cause this nigga Bocka takes pride in his work," Dolph chimed back in.

"Word?" Chyna asked, pointing the piece at different walls inside the basement, imagining himself blowing mothafuckaz away.

"Yeah, not only is the homie a notable shooter, but he's the gunsmith of the family," Dolph told him, taking another sip from his cup. "My guy knows a lot about guns and bullets. Truth of the matter is they both go hand and hand."

"Dat bewtiful lady in ya dick beaters issa gold-plated .45 ACP with a onyx handle," Bocka informed him. "She holds a total of twelve hollow tip rounds of me own creation. You hitta nicca wit somethin' dis exclusive, him ain't neva gettin' him ass up again. Ya hear me?" Bocka smiled and hung his arm around Chyna's shoulders. His eyes were laser-focused on the young nigga fooling around with the gold-plated pistol.

"I think I'm in love…blowl, bowl, blowl, blowl!" Chyna said, making gunshot sounds as he pointed the golden gun in different directions.

"Who ya callin' dere, King?" Bocka asked, throwing his head back like *What's up?*

Dolph, who was holding his cellphone, looked up at him wearing a smile on his lips. "Makin' arrangements for the ceremony, kid. You know how the Kings do."

CHAPTER NINE

Chyna wasn't sweating, not getting a piece of the action, he was happy to get his ink and become an official member of the royal crime family. Dolph made a phone call to his brother, King Morpheus to get an okay to bring Chyna into the fold. Chyna chopped it up with King Morpheus for a time so he'd have an understanding of what he was getting into. The phone call ended with King Morpheus welcoming him into their organization.

Chyna got his tattoo done by one of the Kings of Thieves. Dolph and Bocka made sure he was good and wasted before he'd gotten the official brand. Under the influence of alcohol the needle of the tattoo gun felt like the annoying stinging of bumble bees over and over again. Once Chyna had finished being tagged, the tattoo artist, a Spanish kid who everyone called Graffiti, wrapped his arm in Saniderm, which was a medical-grade, waterproof tattoo bandage.

Chyna was then blindfolded and driven to the destination where the ceremony was to take place. He was taken to a dark, cold room with cobblestone walls that were lit by torches. There were two rows of men standing on either side of Chyna wearing hooded, purple cloaks with gold ropes tied around their waists. Chyna was told to walk down the center of these men until he was told to stop. He did exactly what he was told until a loud, authority-filled voice commanded him.

"Stop!" The voice rang out thunderously."Remove your blindfold, king."

Chyna removed his blindfold. His eyes narrowed from the torches' lights as he looked around the room. The place gave him sinister cult-like vibes and made him feel like he had all kinds of creepy crawlies climbing over him. He smacked his arm and scratched but there wasn't anything there. Once his sight adjusted to the light, he focused his attention on the man before him that commanded him to stop. The man was wearing the hood of a purple cloak and a gold rope around his waist also. His face couldn't be seen at all. It was completely dark. He looked creepy as fuck to Chyna but he was sure who it was beneath the hood.

The man lifted his jeweled hands and removed his hood. He lifted his head and looked at Chyna. His milky-white eye made an icy chill slide down Chyna's back. No matter how many times he'd seen that nigga Dolph without glasses, he'd never get used to that creepy ass eye of his.

"Kings, remove your hoods!" Dolph commanded the members of his royal crime family. One by one, the members removed their hoods and revealed their identity. The group was composed mostly of Blacks and Latinos. There were also Asians and Whites sprinkled here and there throughout the collective. "King Bocka and I would like to nominate our protégé Chyna for membership among the royal family. Let anyone who is not in agreement of our decision, speak now or forever hold yo' peace." He took in all the faces of the members present, and not a soul among them opposed Chyna joining their sacred society. "Good. Let the ceremony begin."

53

Dolph looked down at the podium at a black box with a shiny gold skull on it wearing a crown. He removed a gold necklace from around his neck containing a gold skeleton key. He unlocked the box and opened its lid. Inside there was a gold rhinestone cup and a gold dagger with a matching skull on its hilt.

Dolph went on to explain what the Kings of Thieves organization was all about and then he told Chyna their rules and regulations. Once he was sure his protégé had a clear understanding of everything, he called the members up one by one. He poked each one of them in their palm and blood poured out of their wound into the rhinestone cup. By the time he'd gotten finished, the cup was halfway filled so he passed it to Chyna.

Chyna was disgusted by the mixture of plasma inside of the rhinestone cup. His stomach did somersaults and he wanted to vomit. But his wanting to be inducted into the ranks of the criminal organization so badly made him keep down what he'd eaten earlier.

"Drink, young king, and become one with your peers," Dolph told him, placing his hand on his shoulder. "Drink and become one with us all. Drink and become our blood brother—drink and become royalty—drink and become a King." Chyna nodded understandingly and guzzled down the plasma. His face balled up from the copper taste and he wiped his wet mouth with the back of his fist.

Dolph took the cup away from him and set it aside. Using one hand, he motioned for Chyna to lower himself to one knee and bow his head. He lifted the gold dagger, touched either of Chyna's shoulders, and then touched the dagger upon the top of his head.

"I, King Dolph, by the powers vested in me, here by crown you, King Chyna," Dolph told him and placed the gold dagger back inside of the black box. He then extended his hand to Chyna. "Rise to your feet, King Chyna, and embrace your brothers." Chyna rose to his feet, shaking up with all of the Kings of Thieves and then hugging them.

Dolph called up the sister organization to the Kings of Thieves, Queens of Thieves. When the ladies came through shit really got popping. There was alcohol, weed and every drug a nigga could name available for those in attendance. Some of the hottest Hip-Hop songs from the 90's and the mid-2000's were played while a few of the Queens ground on each other and on some of the Kings. Some of the Queens had gotten so loaded they stripped to their panties and danced provocatively on the table tops. The Kings cheered them on and threw dollars at them. Once everything had wound down, they talked among each other playing Spades, shooting craps and vibing to good music.

Chyna sat on the arm of the couch with a Heineken bottle dangling between his legs. Anyone looking at him could tell he was White Boy Wasted from his lowered-eyes and goofy look on his face. Regardless of his being inebriated, he was still able to hold a conversation with Bocka without slurring his words.

"Me tellin' you, youth, dere's big, big money out here for da takin'. Ya got down just in time with da right kinda crew so you stand ta make a fortune out here, ya hear me, brudda?" Bocka asked with a blunt as long and as wide as a tampon wedged between his fingers. He had a thick, light-skinned joint occupying his lap with her arm stretched around his shoulders. He shared his big ass blunt with her while rubbing and squeezing her juicy thigh.

"No doubt. I'm hungry as a hostage so I'm tryna eat everythang in sight. Nah mean?" Chyna asked, reaching underneath his shirt and rubbing his chest.

Bocka blew out a cloud as he passed the wafting blunt back to shorty sitting on his lap. He nodded to what Chyna had just said.

"Me feel ya. Me feel ya, nicca," Bocka said. He looked across the room and saw Dolph hollering at one of the Queens of Thieves he knew by the name of Devon. "But feel dis, brudda, me and da nicca Dolph go way back. Me talkin' way, way back, ya hear me? Me love all me bruddas like dey came from da same womb as me." Chyna nodded as he took a swig of his beer. "I mean no disrespect when I tell ya dis, youth, but should ya ever cross us, me gonna come after you, nicca, and me gonna kill you in dee most brutalist way me can think of."

Chyna was about to take another drink of his beer when Bocka stated this. He didn't like the thought of being threatened by anyone. He started to bust the beer bottle over the Rasta's head but held fast.

"Bocka, I understand where you're comin' from but I ain't feelin' being threatened and shit," Chyna told him.

Bocka took the blunt from shorty on his lap before responding. "No disrespect, none whatsoever, me got love for ya, youth. Just consider what me say a warning or sorts. Ya hemme?" He went on to take a few puffs of the blunt and blow out a cloud. He tried to pass the blunt to Chyna but he threw up a hand, letting him know he was good.

"Young king, what that shit do?" Dolph approached with a smile across his face. He had a double styrofoam cup of that purple shit in one hand while his arm was around the shoulders of little mama he was having dialogue with earlier.

"Whatever I tell it to. Who this?" Chyna asked, taking shorty in from head to toe. She was a five-foot-three number with B-cup breasts and an ass and hip ratio fit to saddle up and ride. She had slanted-eyes, skin the color of honey and a cute face sprinkled with freckles. Her long, cherry-blonde hair spilled from beneath a purple bandana that matched perfectly with her purple and black plaid shirt. The shirt was tied just below her tits, boasting her ample cleavage and diamond navel piercing.

"My bad, king, where are my manners? This lovely young lady goes by the name, Queen Devon," Dolph said, turning Devon around in a 380-degree turn with one hand, letting Chyna see just how stacked she was. The young nigga couldn't help ogling her and biting down on his bottom lip. "Devon, meet the newest addition to our family, King Chyna."

Devon smiled sexily at Chyna and extended her manicured hand. "Pleasure to meet chu, King Chyna."

"Oh, the pleasure is all mine, ma," Chyna replied, kissing Devon on her hand.

"Queen, why don't chu welcome my man here to the kingdom properly," Dolph said, taking a drink from his styrofoam cups.

"With pleasure," Devon licked her pouty-lips with her pierced tongue. She grasped Chyna's hand and led him away. He plucked a gold foil-wrapped condom from Dolph's fingers as he walked past him.

Dolph took another drink from his styrofoam cups as he turned to watch Chyna and Devon make their way through the crowd. "Look at my young nigga, happier than a pig in shit," he smiled. "Where you going, Bocka?" He frowned, seeing Bocka being led past him by the shorty that had been sitting on his lap.

"You mean, where are we goin'?" Shorty answered for Bocka, taking Dolph by his hand and leading him away with them.

"Chooochooooo!" Dolph mimicked the sounds of a train.

CHAPTER TEN

Bartise wore a look of concentration as he trained with his escrima sticks, in the backyard of his mansion. He was so far gone in his session, the six bikini clad beauties playing in his pool were not a distraction for him.

"The champ is here! The champ is here! The champ is here!" Hamza said over and over again, drumming on his hairy chest. He had swelling under his right eye and a busted lip from the fight he was in hours ago, but it wasn't a big deal to him. He'd walked away victorious and a few thousand dollars richer.

Bartise turned around connecting the escrima sticks, to form a staff. A smirk spread across his face seeing Hamza, Purp and Stutter-Box approaching him. Purp and Stutter-Box were toting two Louis Vuitton travel bags each so he knew Hamza had done his thing.

"I won't even bother asking how we did, seeing how happy this nigga is," Bartise said, stabbing his staff into the ground. His forehead wrinkled when he looked among the men and didn't see his lady. "Where's lil' mama?"

"She—she—she went—went—" Stutter-Box struggled to spit it out.

"This nigga, son, I don't even know why he even tries," Purp interjected, shaking his head. "Shorty went upstairs, said she was tired."

Stutter-Box threw up his middle finger and Purp mouthed "fuck you" back at him.

"How is she lookin' on her end?" Bartise asked about the loot Chrissy made that night at the strip club.

"Man, now you know that I know that you don't want niggaz poking their nose in yo' business, especially when it comes to money," Purp replied.

Bartise grinned and said, "Of course I know. I was just checkin' to see if you're on yo' shit or not." He patted him on his shoulder.

"Look—look—look at this—this nigga, man." Stutter-Box nodded toward the pool. When Purp and Bartise looked over their shoulder, they saw Hamza stipping down to his underwear and then cannonball diving in the pool. He then started wrestling with a couple of the women.

"It's all good. Homie deserves it," Bartise said, with his eyes on Hamza.

"You ain't never lied, B. Ya man brought that bag in, ya heard?" Purp said, lifting up both the Louis Vuitton travel bags. "Real shit. That Sand Nigga been running through the competition. Bruh ain't lost a single fight."

"I know. That's why I plan on bookin' his next fight real, real soon," Bartise told him. "I'm telling you, Purp, all I need is about three or four more thumpin' ass niggaz like 'em and the god will be a billionaire."

"A billionaire? Mannnn, get the fuck outta here," Purp smirked.

"Oh, he of lil' faith, have you not seen what I've accomplished in such a short time?" Bartise grinned as he opened his arms and made a 360-degree turn. Purp took in the mega mansion he'd purchased. The place was humongous, sitting on 100-acres. It was all white, with a fountain and the most gorgeous rose bushes out front. Bartise had hired ex-cartel hitmen as security, the most vicious Dobermann Pinschers as guard dogs, and saw to it that all the mansion's staff were strapped.

"I ain't never beena nigga to front. You did that so salute, my G." Purp nodded. He'd been down with Bartise from the beginning so he'd witnessed his come up.

"Thank you." Bartise gave him a short bow.

"Here—here—I—I come!" Stutter-Box yelled.

Purp and Bartise looked toward the pool, to see Stutter-Box in his boxer briefs doing a front flip into the water. He swam back up to the surface and started playing around with the women.

Bartise turned back around shaking his head. He stepped out of the way as Purp ran past him, leaving a trail of clothes in his wake. He was making hurried footsteps towards the pool.

"These niggaz, bruh." Bartise smiled before contacting his maids through his earpiece. Promptly, the two women scurried outside picking up the Louis Vuitton travel bags. "Ladies, I'd like for you to count that purse and leave the bags on the desk inside of my study. I'll put it away myself. Thank you."

"No problem, Mr. Glover," the maids said in unison as they headed back to the mansion.

Bartise looked up at Chrissy's bedroom window to find her staring down at him. He held her gaze for a while before smiling and blowing her a kiss. Chrissy let the curtain fall back over the window and turned out the lights in her bedroom.

The screams and hollers coming from the pool drew Bartise's attention over his shoulder. Hamza, Purp and Stutter-Box looked like they were having the time of their lives and he didn't want to miss out on all of the fun. Bartise removed his earpiece and stripped down to his silk underwear. He ran towards the pool and dove inside.

***

Chrissy showered, wrapped her hair up in a scarf and slipped on the t-shirt Jayvon had given her some time ago. She loved the fact that it still held his scent. It made her feel like he was in the bedroom with her then. Chrissy picked up the framed photo of her, Jayvon and Chyna that they'd taken at a carnival on the Coney Island Boardwalk. A smile graced her face as she thought about the ball her and the boys had that night. She'd never had so much fun in her life.

"My lil' family. Man, I love y'all so, so much," Chrissy said, tracing Jayvon's and Chyna's faces. She kissed them both then sat the framed photograph on the nightstand beside her bed.

Chrissy turned out the lamp light and snuggled under the covers. She'd just drifted off to sleep when Bartise and his company's racket woke her back up. With all the noise they were making, anyone listening would have sworn on a stack of Bibles there were some wild ass fraternity party taking place. Chrissy knew she wouldn't get any rest if she had to listen to that shit all night. So she put in her Airpods and started the playlist she made that reminded her of Jayvon.

Chrissy shut her eyes and allowed her mind to carry her away to Jayvon. In addition to all of the good times they shared, she thought about their interaction back at the hotel regarding Bartise. She knew without a doubt her boo would go against one of the most feared gangstas in the city behind her and she loved him for it. But Bartise was an entirely different breed of monster. She could never shake the thoughts of what she saw him do to the women who tried to escape his rule, without paying what he called the proper compensation. One incident stuck out in her mind like a sore thumb. This particular young lady was one of the sister wives but she had become like a sister to her. She tried to coerce Chrissy into fleeing Bartise's mansion with her but something told her to stay put. Chrissy was grateful she'd followed the advice of that tiny voice in the back of her head, because what she witnessed Bartise do to Ophelia was something that would make even the likes of the devil cringe.

CHAPTER ELEVEN

Ophelia stood over a yellow cake spreading chocolate frosting over it. Her man, Kanan, held her waist from behind, kissing on the side of her neck. She smiled and giggled. Ophelia licked the frosting off the big wooden spoon and then passed it to Kanan. He rubbed the chocolate frosting on the side of her neck and began to lick on it. His licking eventually turned to sucking. Ophelia closed her eyes and began to moan. Her panties dampened from her arousal. Bending over, she stuck out her firm, round ass and felt Kanan's hardened manhood pressed against her. Before she knew it he was tugging her panties down her thighs and pumping his one-eyed snake.

Ophelia gripped the sides of the stove and wagged her booty from side to side. Looking over her shoulder at Kanan, she made her ass bounce and clap vigorously. Enticed by the show, he licked his fingers and rubbed her rigid clit in a circle. Ophelia's forehead wrinkled. Her eyes narrowed. She bounced and clapped her cheeks faster.

"Damn, shorty," Kanan said under his breath, slipping two fingers inside of her warm, wet hole and jabbing it rapidly. Ophelia threw her head back, hollering, and shaking like a vibrator. Her essence burst from her sex and rained on the floor. Kanan smacked both of Ophelia's buttocks hard and fast, leaving red hand impressions behind. She yelped and shook again. That freak shit turned her horny ass on! "You like that shit, huh? You like when Big Daddy smacks that lil' fat ass of yours? Huh?"

"Oh, yes, yes, Daddy," Ophelia whined, licking her top lip and displaying her tongue ring. *Kanan kneeled down, spread her ass cheeks open and came face to face with her crinkle. Closing his eyes, he pressed his nose against her brown-eye and sniffled it like it was a line of coke. Her natural scent put a smile on his lips and made him shiver with arousal.*

Kanan spat on Ophelia's booty hole and flicked his tongue across it rapidly. Pleasured noises slipped from between her lips. She backed her butt further onto his mouth as he began sucking and munching her hidden jewel. She slipped her manicured hand between her thighs and rubbed her clit in a circular motion. Her bald kitty contracted and expelled more of her juices.

"Mmmmmm," Kanan devoured Ophelia's booty hole hungrily. The sound of his eating her from behind turned her on to no end.

"Daddy—Daddy—" Ophelia called Kanan soft and sensually.

"Yes...baby..." Kanan replied between munching her hole, looking like he was French Kissing it.

"I want chu to fuck me—I want chu to fuck me in my asssss," Ophelia said in a soft, sensual voice.

Kanan feasted on her booty a while longer before standing up and wiping his mouth. He treated her butt cheeks like they were drums, slapping his pole against them. Biting down on his bottom lip, Kanan pressed his small head against the entrance of her backdoor. He was about to slam it down to his hairy ball sack when he heard a Ba-Boom!

"Oh, shiiit!" Kanan's eyes lit up when he saw three masked men enter the house. He pulled his boxer briefs up and ran out of the kitchen. He was fast! It was just too bad the bullets from one of the masked men's guns were even faster. Kanon's face twisted in agony as hot slugs melted into his back. He fell awkwardly to the floor, squirming like a fish out of water until the shooter ended his suffering—forever.

Choot! Choot!

"Nooooooo! Nooooooo!" Ophelia screamed horrifically when she saw the masked man pop two in her lover's knot. She fled the kitchen with hopes of making an escape before she could be gunned down. She cut past one of the masked men who was wearing a Nike tracksuit. Before she could clear his path, he tripped her and she collided with the living room floor. Wincing, she held her aching side and attempted to get up again.

"You know, I usually send a couple of my guys to handle situations like this, but when one of my ladies runs away, I take it very, very personally. So the god had to tag along on this housecall. Nah mean?" The masked man, in the Nike tracksuit said, unzipping his jacket and brandishing an escrima stick. As soon as Ophelia heard his voice, she knew exactly who he was. She was so choked up with terror she found difficulty in saying his name.

"Bar—Bar—Bartise?" Ophelia *finally managed.*

"That's right, ho, it's me, and look who I've brought along," Bartise replied, pulling off his ski

mask and shaking his dreadlocks free. He took the time to run his fingers through his hair.

"D—Damage," Ophelia uttered the escrima stick name as soon as she saw it. She could have sworn she heard its victims crying for help on some paranormal shit. All the women who'd run a foul of Bartise had their names carved into the stick. Ophelia was assaulted by flashbacks of the countless women she'd seen bludgeoned to death with Damage. The barbaric nature in which the ladies were murdered had left her suffering from PTSD.

Bartise smiled wickedly as he patted the escrima stick into his palm. Ophelia's cheeks ballooned as she tried to hold back bile. She threw up and then farted. Little mama was as nervous as a mouse cornered by a snake in its enclosure.

"Make sure you record alla this shit. I want Chrissy to see what will happen to her lil' pretty ass should she ever try to leave me." Bartise told Purp. Not long after Kanan had been slumped, he pulled out his iPhone and started recording the chaos.

"I gotchu faded," Purp assured him, focusing his cellphone on what was about to unfold.

Ophelia's cheeks flooded with tears and she held up her trembling hand. "Daddy, please, please, I—"

"Ooooh, now, I'm Daddy? Fuck happened to Bartise, bitch?" Bartise scowled, cutting her pleas short.

"Daddy, I'm—"

Crackkkk!

The escrima stick slammed into Ophelia's temple, snapping her head to the side. She fell on her side with a bloody indention on the side of her dome.

Her eyes were rolled to their whites. She was shaking crazily and foaming at the mouth. Purp and Stutter-Box watched as their boss beat the poor girl savagely. He took Damage to every exposed part of her body. Blood clung to the carpet and everything else inside the living room.

"Whooo!" Bartise threw his head back, shouting like a drunk college white boy. "Boy, am I parched. I could use a drinky drink," he addressed Purp and Stutter-Boy, "How about y'all? Y'all niggaz thirsty?" They shook their heads, no.

Bartise hoisted the bloody escrima stick over his shoulder as he walked in the kitchen. He opened the refrigerator, grabbed a Budweiser, popped off its cap and downed half of it. Belching, he rinsed the blood from his escrima stick and dried it off. He then sat his beer down and snatched a butcher's knife from out of one of the drawers. He held his stick down with one hand and used the other to carve Ophelia's name into it. Afterwards, he blew the residue off the escrima stick, hoisted it over his shoulder like a baseball bat and walked out of the kitchen.

Bartise glanced at Stutter-Box who was kneeling over Ophelia checking for a pulse.

"She's—she's stilla—stilla live," Stutter-Box reported, gripping his gun with the silencer on its barrel. "You—you—you want—want me to—to putta—putta outta her m—misery?"

"If you want to Stutter, I really don't give a shit," Bartise told him on his way out the door. "The bitch can lie there suffering until she meets the cold hands of death for all I care. Y'all niggaz hurry up and meet

me back at the whip, whatever you decide to do." He disappeared through the door, leaving Stutter-Box and Purp behind in the house. He'd gotten halfway across the yard when he heard the soft whispers of Stutter-Box's gun.

***

When Chrissy's eyes popped open she saw Bartise standing at the forefront of eight women. They were all partially hidden in the darkness. Although she couldn't see their faces she knew they were all of the sister wives Bartise had murdered. Frightened, Chrissy jumped out of bed and stumbled back against the wall. She wore a face of fear as she took in all of the sister wives standing before her. Chrissy dropped her head and squeezed her eyes shut. When she looked back up Bartise and the sister wives had vanished. Her brows furrowed wondering what had just happened to her. She removed the Airpods from her ears, placed them on the nightstand and sat down on the bed. She recalled something Bartise had told her after she'd viewed the footage of him murdering Ophelia.

Once mine. Always mine. Until I say otherwise.

"God willing. I'm gonna get outta here. I have to," Chrissy said under her breath before lying back in bed. She took a deep breath and closed her eyes.

CHAPTER TWELVE

Chyna lay across the bed in his boxer briefs and socks. His hands were interlocked behind his head as he watched Devon undress at the foot of the bed. Devon reached behind her back and unclasped her bra. She removed it and slung it aside. She slipped off her panties and kicked them aside as well. Next, she climbed upon the bed and crawled towards Chyna like a leopard looking to pounce on its prey.

Devon kissed Chyna slowly and passionately. They swiped their tongues across each other and then she sucked on his. She kissed him again, sucking on his bottom lip and planting soft kisses down his chest. Licking his lips, Chyna closed his eyes and moaned under his breath. His nipples stiffened. Devon used her tongue to trace his old wounds and keloid scars. Then, she kissed them tenderly. She gently bit down the trail of hair that led down to the waistband of his boxer briefs. Her breath tickled the small trail of hairs on his abs and excited him. His piece grew and grew until it formed a tint inside of his underwear.

Devon peeled off Chyna's boxer briefs and slung them aside. She was pleased by his endowment. It was long and masculine-looking with veins running up and down it. She tugged it up and down making it go stronger and longer. She smacked its head and its shaft against her face while moaning sensually. Chyna gasped and his stomach muscles clenched. He was so hard that a clear gel-like bubble formed at his pee hole and rolled down the side of his meat. Devon expanded her jaws like an anaconda and engulfed every inch of him. She massaged his nut sack as she bobbed up and down his dick, using her free hand to jack him. Gagging and slurping noises invaded the bedroom. A hot coat of saliva ran over his manhood and down his balls. His eyes rolled back in his head. His mouth hung open. He gripped her head while she attempted to suck his soul out of him.

"Aaaaah, fuck. Ssssss, nasty ass bitch!" Chyna stole a glance at Devon, her eyes were glued on him.

Devon popped his dick out of her mouth and smacked his piece against her cheek. "Only for you, lil' daddy," she said, stuffing his meat back inside of her mouth. He buried the back of his head into the pillow. He clenched his teeth and listened to her sloppy blowjob. Her sensual moaning turned him on so much he swore his dick expanded in length and width.

Devon popped Chyna's pipe out of her mouth, leaving a string of shiny saliva from her bottom lip to his bulbous head. Standing up on her knees, she wiped her mouth as she continued to pump his engorged penis. As if by magic, the gold-foil MAGNUM condom appeared in her hand and she pulled it open with her teeth. She slipped the slippery rubber out of its packaging and used her mouth to slide it over his pole. She climbed upon him, reached back, and guided his piece into her warm pocket. Grasping his pecks, she licked her lips and shut her eyes. She started off winding her hips slowly then she gradually sped up, making his endowment crash into her walls. Chyna's eyes turned into slits and he bit down on his bottom lip. He grasped her waist as she ground into him, riding him like a cowboy would a wild bull.

"Ooooooou, shit, lil' daddy," Devon gasped, clicking her tongue against the roof of her mouth. That young dick was feeling amazing to her. It was brushing against sensitive spots inside of her she didn't know existed. She was getting wetter and wetter by the second. She began winding her hips faster and making the sexiest noises Chyna had ever heard in his life. He could bust off hearing them alone.

Not one to be out performed, Chyna smacked her on her ass and instructed her to lay down on her stomach. He slipped his brick inside of her, held her wrists behind her back and began fucking her hard. She squeezed her eyes closed and hollered into the mattress like she was being brutally murdered. Chyna grunted and sweated profusely, jabbing his piece in and out of her rapidly.

"Yeah, bitch, take this dick, take every muthafuckin' inch of it!" Chyna said, looking like a madman, droplets of sweat splashing on Devon's back. He grabbed a fistful of her hair, pulled her head back and continued to fuck her brains out. What looked like shaving cream oozed out of Devon's pussy and partially lathered the latex hugging Chyna's piece.

"Oh, yes, yeah! Fuck me, baby! Fuck me like a dirty lil' slut! Oooooou!" Devon whined with her eyes closed and her mouth open. Chyna was stuffing her yellow-ass like a Thanksgiving turkey and he wasn't showing any signs of slowing down.

"Who this pussy belong to? Huh? Who this muthafuckin' pussy belong to?" Chyna asked, pummeling that coochie like a pornstar.

"Aaah, Chyna! Chyna, goddamn!" Devon hollered blissfully.

Chyna flipped Devon over on her back, wiped the sweat from his brow and pulled her into him. He tapped his manhood against her clit. Then he pressed it against it and rubbed it fast. Devon squirmed and moaned. Her eyes rolled back and her mouth hung open. Her voice rose higher and higher. Then the sound went out and then it came back again. She shook hard and started squirting like crazy.

"Ooooooooh, shhiiiiiiiiit!" Devon pulled the sheets and bit into her left shoulder. Her entire body shook as if she was in a massage chair.

Chyna slid his endowment into Devon's warm pocket before mashing her breasts together and sucking on her nipples at the same time. She slipped her hands between her legs and rubbed her swollen clitoris. The combination of Chyna sucking and fucking her while she manipulated her womanhood, pushed her toward her orgasm. Again, she shook like crazy and then laid flat out on the bed. Chyna sat up groping her breasts and giving her long strokes. She moaned softly, feeling herself approach another climax. She looked up at Chyna and began playing with his nipples. Surprisingly, he liked it. He narrowed his eyes and licked his lips. He sped up his stroking and his groping of her breasts.

Devon's eyes rolled to the back of her head, her nostrils flared and she gasped. To be so young Chyna had a mean up and down game and it was driving her wild. Still, she required more if she was ever going to reach that level of orgasmic explosion.

"Deeper, deeper, deeper, deeper," Devon whined.

"Deeper, huh? You want me to fuck the shit outta you?" Chyna asked, grabbing her by her neck roughly. He shook her hard and made her hair fall over her face. She smiled wickedly and egged him on.

"Yeah. Yes. Fuck me, fuck me, fuck me like a dirty lil' slut," Devon told him, as he pounded her. Chyna's face balled up and he went at her harder and harder. His stroking seemed to make Devon wetter than a Slip-N-Slide.

"Oh, you wanna be fucked like a slut? I gotchu. I gotchu, bitch," Chyna frowned and squared his jaws.

"Yeeaaaah." Devon laughed maniacally and spat in Chyna's face. He hawked up mucus and spat right back in the bitch face.

Chyna laid on top of Devon, slipped his hands underneath her and lifted her buttocks upwards. She wrapped her arms around his neck and opened her legs wider. He sucked and bit on the side of her neck as he stroked her with a vengeance. He went as deep as he could, hitting that G-spot and making her call out his name. His back muscles and buttocks flexed as he drove in and out of her. More and more of her cream gushed out of her and slid onto the sheet.

Devon whined louder and louder as Chyna hit her with strong, rapid, circular strokes. He plunged deeper inside of her, trying to knock the bottom out of her fine ass. His nuts swelled, his manhood fattened, he could feel himself about to explode. He lapped at her faster and faster, making the mattress squeak. His thrust was driving her across the bed and pulling the sheets from off its corners.

"Oh, yes. Oh, God. Don't—don't stop. I'm finna cum—I'm finna—" Devon announced before her face got stuck in a mold of her attempting to scream. She went quiet and still. Chyna continued to hump her with reckless abandon.

"Unh, unh, unh." Chyna grunted, feverishly stroking Devon, making the mattress squeak louder and louder. Sweat beaded on his forehead and slid down his face and back. "Aah, aaah, I'm finna bust—shit. I'm finna bust. Gaaah!" Chyna thrust a few more times before he spilled his hot babies into the beige rubber and collapsed on top of Devon. He lay his head on her chest, breathing so hard one would think he'd ran a marathon. Devon threw her arms and legs around him. She ran her fingers through his wild curly hair, kissed the top of his head, and closed her eyes.

"You have nice, long, beautiful hair, you know that?" Devon asked with her eyes closed.

Chyna took a deep breath. "Unh, huh."

"You should lemme braid it before you go."

"Okay. Just gemme like five more minutes. Cool?"

"Cool." She smiled and kissed the top of his head again.

***

Eight minutes later, Devon and Chyna showered and got dressed in the same clothes they'd worn before they fucked. Devon parted his hair and braided it into six neat cornrows. She then led him inside of the bathroom so he could take a look at it in the medicine cabinet mirror.

Chyna turned from left to right taking in his new look. A smile spread across his face as he rubbed his hands together and continued to admire his hairstyle. He couldn't front, he was definitely feeling the cornrows. He could never find anyone to braid his shit for a price he could afford. So he usually wore it in a messy bun or all over his head.

Devon smiled as she hugged him from behind, staring at both of their reflections in the mirror. "I guess it's safe to say you like the queen's work, huh?"

"No doubt," Chyna replied.

"I figured that," Devon said, tapping her cheek for a kiss. Chyna obliged her and she led him out of the bathroom.

Chyna and Devon emerged from the bedroom to a round of applause from everyone at the party. They smiled, feeling like a celebrity couple at a red carpet event. Dolph emerged from the sea of guests with a blunt of Jamaica's finest hanging from his lips. In his hands was his own gold cable link chain with an icy K and a crown sitting tilted on top of it.

"I got some thangs I want chu to have, king, starting with this," Dolph slipped behind Chyna and latched the gold cable around his neck.

"Yo, son, ain't this yo' shine?" Chyna asked, looking down at the cable and admiring the piece.

Dolph passed him his blunt and he went right to puffing on it. "Yep. You're my protege so I want chu to have it."

"Man, thanks, Dolph. I don't really know what to say," Chyna said stunned, with everyone watching him and his big homie.

"You ain't gotta say nothin', Dunn. Just hold ya manz down and make me proud," Dolph replied, blessing him with the latest iPhone and a little cash.

"Say no more." Chyna shook up with him and gave him a thug hug. The entire room erupted into applause and cheers. Chyna kicked it at the function a while longer before calling it a night.

***

The burger spot was closed and nearly all of its lights were out. Jayvon worked his way down the corridor mopping the floor. A smile was plastered on his face as thoughts of Chrissy were on his mind. He loved the shit out of that girl. There wasn't any doubt in his mind she was going to be his wife someday. Once they'd gotten her out of this situation with Bartise, he planned on saving up enough dough for a ring and popping the big question.

Jayvon laughed when he heard his boss Augustus singing a Curtis Mayfield song down the hall. He wrung out the mop, set the wet floor sign down and crept towards his office. He had it in mind to give him a hard time about his god awful singing. Jayvon was about to give the old man shit when he caught a glimpse of him through the crack of his office door. Still crooning, Augustus removed a portrait of his family off the wall, revealing a safe. Once he'd gotten the safe open, he placed the day's take inside of it.

Man, it's gotta be at least two, three hunnit thousand there. That kinda dough would definitely knock a chunk outta the amount I need to buy Chris back from Bartise bitch-ass, Jayvon thought. He watched Augustus store the calculator, the ink pen and the small black book inside of the safe before closing its door. Next, he shoved his piece inside of the worn leather holster on his hip. He fixed his apple jack on his head and slipped on his jacket. As he reached to turn out the lamp on his desk, Jayvon crept away to put up the mop and bucket. He then sat at one of the tables in the front of the establishment and pretended to be scrolling through his cellphone.

Augustus emerged from his office singing and twirling his key ring around his finger. "Young blood, it's time to roll," he told Jayvon as he walked past him. He unlocked the door and held it open, motioning for him to walk out. "Lady's first, sweetheart."

Jayvon grinned and shook his head at Augustus's antics.

CHAPTER THIRTEEN

Augustus was bumping Otis Reddings' *Try a Little Tenderness* when he pulled up across the street from a row of brownstones. He switched hands with his cigar to throw his vehicle in park and turned down his stereo.

"You needa stop smokin' them bogus ass cigars, man. Them muthafuckaz stank, for real, for real," Jayvon told him. Augustus blew smoke out of his nose as he held up the middle finger. "Good looking out on the ride. I'll see yo' old ass tomorrow." He touched fists with Augustus and hopped out of the truck. He slammed the door shut and hustled across the street.

Augustus let his truck idle as he waited for Jayvon to get in his house safely. This was one of the most dangerous parts of Brooklyn so it was best to be strapped. He took a good look at his surroundings before drawing his pistol from its holster. He cocked the hammer on the shiny piece and laid it on his lap. He then went back to smoking his cigar while taking in the scenery. He sat up in his seat when he saw Jayvon walking upon a purple and gold Mercedes-Benz G-Wagon, parked in front of his brownstone. The tinted windows of the vehicle cracked open, releasing heavy weed smoke and the latest Yo Gotti song.

Jayvon turned around to see Chyna climbing out of the whip with a Gucci knapsack over his shoulder, looking like your typical high school student. Jayvon could tell the little nigga was high as Mars. His eyes were glassy and red-webbed and he had this goofy ass look on his face, like he always did when he was faded.

"Good lookin' out, yo'," Chyna said, throwing up the hand that held his cellphone.

"I know you fuckin' lyin'!" A scowling Jayvon spat angrily before grabbing Chyna's arm and taking a closer look at his K.O.T tattoo.

"Shit," Chyna said under his breath, snatching his arm away.

"Bro, I told you I didn't want chu hangin' around these niggaz," Jayvon said, wagging his finger in his face. He looked up at the whip Chyna was driven home in, to see Dolph and Bocka hopping out.

Chyna scrunched his face. "My nigga, you not gon' keep me on a short leash like I'ma fuckin' dog. I'm damn near a grown man."

Jayvon ignored him and stepped before Dolph. "And you, nigga, I told you to stay the fuck away from my family!"

Dolph frowned confusingly, and looked over both his shoulders. He was trying to see who the fuck Jayvon thought he was talking to.

"My nigga," Dolph began, smacking his hands together. Anyone looking could tell he was trying not to lose his cool. "I've given you a pass lettin' you talk to me out the side of yo' neck our last few encounters, on the strength of baby bro, but let this be the last time you come at a King, or I'll forget how much love I got for yo' bro and let my man, Bocka here,"—He hung his arm around Bocka's shoulders—"blow yo' fuckin' face off. Ya dig?" He smiled at first, but then his face quickly twisted into a mad dog stare. Bocka, mad dogging him as well, upped his pistol, sideways. When Chyna saw this, he stepped in front of his brother to shield him from any danger. They both knew Bocka was a killer. Only it didn't matter to Jayvon. He was so prideful he'd go up against a bullet before backing down from him or anyone else.

"Yo, yo, yo, Bocka chill, son. This my bro," Chyna told him.

Jayvon stared Bocka down fearlessly. "The sight of that gun ain't pumpin' no fear in this here heart. You're gonna have to show and prove, Billy Badass."

"Me hear ya, king, if ya love 'em you better tell 'em somethin' 'fore me buck his black-ass down." Though Bocka was speaking to Chyna, his glare was focused on Jayvon. The tension between them was thick and things could pop off at any moment.

Chyna's heart was beating hard and his palms began to sweat. He found himself stuck between a rock and a hard place. He loved his brother and his street family just the same but it looked like he was going to be forced to make a decision. Slowly, he slid his hand around to the small of his back where he'd tucked the .45 Bocka gave him. His brows dipped when he didn't feel the handle of his pistol.

Jayvon upped Chyna's gold-plated .45 and pulled his brother behind him. "Whatever you 'bout, I'm 'bout. It's however you wanna play it, nigga."

The silence between Jayvon and Bocka seemed to last for an eternity. They wondered which one of them would be the first to die, and in about five more seconds they would find out.

"Relax, king, let the young nigga keep his life," Dolph told Bocka, interrupting what would eventually become a fatal gun battle. Bocka and Jayvon stared each other down a while longer before they finally lowered their guns.

"You getta pass, bowi, ya got Dolph ta thank for dat," Bocka told Jayvon.

"Rasta, you can take that pass and stick it up yo' ass," Jayvon replied, tucking the gun at the small of his back and then tapping Chyna. He walked away with Chyna following closely behind. Chyna looked over his shoulder at Dolph and Bocka as he headed towards the brownstone with his brother. Dolph and Bocka watched the brothers a moment longer before disappearing like ghosts.

***

"What I tell you about hangin' with them niggaz, B?" Jayvon spat angrily, smacking the back of Chyna's head as they entered their crib.

Chyna turned around rubbing the back of his stinging head. He wanted to bust his brother dead in his shit but the love he had for him trumped his ill feelings.

Boom!

Jayvon slammed the door so hard the entire tenement shook and a family portrait fell from the wall. He walked up on Chyna as angry as a bull, clenching and unclenching his fists. He and Chyna were standing face to face like boxers in a ring.

"Bruh, I love you like a home cooked meal, but the next time you raise yo' hand to me, you and I are gon' go twelve rounds in this bitch," Chyna swore, holding his brother's glare. Jayvon had grown used to punching on his brother when he undermined him but Chyna was sixteen-years-old now. He wasn't going to let his brother keep handling him like he was some snotty nose kid.

"So, what chu saying?" Jayvon asked, taking the .45 from the small of his back and lying it upon the end table.

Chyna peeped the move so he knew what was up. It was time to get it cracking from the shoulders. He slipped his knapsack off his shoulder and dropped it on the floor. "I think I just said it."

Chyna swung on Jayvon. He ducked it and came back up with a devastating three punch combination. Chyna stumbled backwards, knocking over the end table and bumping up against the door. He touched his lips and his fingertips came away bloody. He looked at Jayvon and he threw up his dukes.

I can't believe this nigga done hit me. His lil' brother. A'ight let's get it then, my nigga, Chyna thought with a bloody mouth. He swallowed it and mad dogged Jayvon. Then he charged at him like he was going to punch him and kicked him in his leg instead. Once Jayvon dropped down to one knee, he followed up with a left and then an overhand right to the face. Chyna went to knee him in the face but he blocked it and lifted him high over his head. Grunting, Jayvon dumped him on the glass coffee table, which exploded in broken glass and splinters. The brothers lay on their backs on opposite sides of each other breathing hard.

"You had enough, or should we go again?" Chyna asked with a sweaty forehead.

"You've gotta be kiddin' me. Son, you still want the fair one after that?" Jayvon looked at him like he was nuts while sweat slid down his forehead.

"I don't play when it comes to my respect. I'm willing to die behind it, Scrap," Chyna confessed.

"I salute cho character, bro," Jayvon saluted him. "You've got mad heart."

"Appreciate that. So what's up? You gon' stop tryna lil' bro me, or do we have to get busy again."

"You're my lil' brother, man. I don't wanna fight chu," Jayvon told him. "I love you. When I hurt chu I hurt me."

"I feel the same way. I wouldn't let nan one of these niggaz out in these streets son me and I'm not about to let chu either," Chyna said.

"I feel you but besides Chris, you're all I got," Jayvon told him, sitting up in the broken glass and splinters. "I lose you to the streets and I'd be all fucked up. You're my lil' man."

"You're not gonna lose me, bro. Come on," Chyna said, shaking off the broken glass and standing up. He extended his hand and pulled Jayvon up. They plucked the broken glass out of each other's hair and clothing. "Are you forgetting about pops? You know we still got him."

"Pops ain't never coming home after all them niggaz he killed."

"He's still our old man, and he's still alive," Chyna told him. "We can't count the old nigga out."

"Yeah. I know." Jayvon walked over to the family portrait that had fallen when he slammed the door behind him. Holding it in both hands, he took a good look at it. It was of him, Chyna and their parents. They'd gotten dressed up in their Sunday's best attire to take the pictures. This one that had gotten framed was his old man's favorite one.

Jayvon hung the portrait back on the wall, making sure it wasn't crooked. Chyna came to stand beside him hanging his arm around his shoulders.

"Those were the good ol' days." Chyna grinned.

"Yeah, that's when we were really a family," Jayvon added with a grin. "Pops had us in all kinda sports and shit. We were always having functions at the house; going to amusement parks and whatnot. Mannn, I'd do anything to get back to those days."

"Yeah. Me, too," Chyna said, taking a deep breath. They stared up at the portrait reminiscing a while longer before he broke their chain of thought. "Anyway, lemme show you what I came up on fucking with Dolph and them niggaz." He nudged Jayvon, grabbed up his knapsack, and motioned for him to follow him inside of the kitchen.

Chyna opened his knapsack and pulled out a freezer bag filled with off white crack rocks. He passed the bag to Jayvon. He held it up to the light and took a good look at its contents.

"How much is this?"

"1000 grams, son. A whole bird."

"A whole bird, huh?" Jayvon sat down at the kitchen table, staring at the freezer bag. "Where'd you get this shit? Are some fools gon' come after you? I needa know what we're up against behind this."

"You ain't gotta worry about that, bro," Chyna pulled out a chair and sat down at the kitchen table. "That nigga Dolph blessed me with that seeing how

I handled business today. Whatever we make off it is ours. I figure we chop the shit up into dimes and pitch 'em. All the money will go to gettin' sis back."

Jayvon looked at his brother with a surprised look on his face. Although neither of them had ever been selfish, Chyna's willingness to give up his share of the profits from the bird said a lot about his character.

"You sho', bro? I mean, that's a lotta dough to be—"

"Yeah, I'm sure. Chrissy is fam. My big sister," Chyna replied, cutting him short. "I love her just as much as you do. We've gotta do whatever we gotta do to get her back."

Jayvon smiled as he rose from his chair. He came around the kitchen table, hugging his brother with one arm and kissing him on the side of the head. "Thanks, Mighty Mouse, this really means a lot to me. I know it will mean lot to Chris also."

"No thanks needed. We do what we have gotta to take care of our own, right?" He looked over his shoulder at him.

"Right," Jayvon agreed with a nod. He turned around to walk out of the kitchen but Chyna's calling after him stopped him short.

"Where are you goin'?" Chyna asked with a wrinkled forehead.

"To get the gloves and stuff so we can start cutting this shit," Jayvon replied. "Do me a favor and grab those sandwich bags off the top of the refrigerator."

"A'ight," Chyna said, taking down the cheap box of sandwich bags.

"Yo, who showed you how to rock this shit up? That nigga Dolph?" Jayvon asked when he returned with the items he'd had in mind and sat down at the kitchen table.

"Yep. You guessed it," Chyna replied, drumming his fingers on the table top.

CHAPTER FOURTEEN

Chyna and Jayvon spent the greater part of the night chopping and bagging up the brick. Jayvon already knew how he could dispose of most of the work if not all of it. He had a clientele of strippers at Big Daddy's that bought all of their weed from him. Anytime they came to shop they'd ask him about crack but he never had any. Come to find out the bitchez liked mixing crack with their weed to get high.

Jayvon thought it was crazy how things worked out. Here he was looking for a plug on some work and out of nowhere his little brother showed up with a whole brick. He looked at this good fortune as God looking out for him. Jayvon planned on selling the work and whatever marijuana he had left to the strippers. He was positive he could move all of his merchandise in a week, week and a half, tops. Chyna agreed with Jayvon's plan to sell their drugs to the clientele at the strip club. He believed in his big brother. If Jayvon said he can make it happen then he was going to make it happen.

Jayvon took his ringing cellphone out of his pocket and checked the caller identification. He expected it to be Chrissy but it was his old man, Trick. He was calling him from a contraband cellular he'd obtained while incarcerated.

"Who is that?" Chyna frowned.

"Pops," Jayvon replied, pulling off his latex gloves.

"Put it on speaker."

Jayvon accepted the call, told his father he was on *speaker* and sat his cellphone on the table.

"What up, old man?" Jayvon started off.

"'Sup, pops? They finally gave yo' asshole a rest so you could call home, huh?" Chyna smiled, hopping upon the table.

Jayvon snickered and playfully shoved his brother.

Trick laughed and said, "I see you got jokes, Mighty Mouse. These fools know betta than to try yo' daddy. This country boy's a beast witta banga and I can thump wit the best of 'em. Shiiiit, I've been scrappin' with niggaz and nigga hatin' crackaz since I was kneehigh to a caterpilla. I'm not locked in here wit these niggaz they're locked in here wit me. Ya heard me?"

Jayvon laughed and said, "Talk yo' shit, pops."

"Pops, who are you kiddin'? You probably snuggled up beside some nigga right now." Chyna grinned.

"Hahahahahahaha! Boy, I swear you've got some mouth on you," Trick told him. "You look like me but act exactly like your m—" he let the rest of the word die in his throat. The jovial expressions vanished from Jayvon and Chyna's faces and an uncomfortable silence filled the kitchen. The word Trick stopped just short of saying was "momma". She was the reason he was locked up for the remainder of his natural life. She'd abandoned their family and broke their hearts so he murdered her and her lover. The boys had unwittingly assisted him in the drills. They were devastated upon learning they had a hand in their mother's demise. It was hard for them to forgive their father but eventually they found it in their hearts.

Jayvon cleared his throat. "So, pops, what's a day like for you in there? What chu do every day?"

"Well, son, they wake us up 'round five in da mornin'..." Trick went on to tell the boys about how he spent most of his days. "Anyway, y'all don't do no dumb shit that'll land y'all in here, where I'm at. Prison is no place for a black man. Hell, it's no place for any man, period. I'm locked up in here like an animal and these white folks feedin' me like I'm one too."

Trick hollered at his sons a while longer before calling it a night. They exchanged "I love you's" before all parties disconnected the call. Jayvon and Chyna stashed the drugs they'd bagged up and crashed on the couch. They watched *The Jeffersons* until they fell asleep.

***

Jayvon's forehead was peppered with sweat as he stood over the grill. He flipped over two sizzling hamburger patties, smacked slices of cheese on them, and tended to the onions he had cooking on the side. Two beads of sweat jetted down the side of his face so he used the collar of his shirt to wipe his face. He sat the spatula aside and grabbed the handle of the metal basket containing the homemade fries. He lifted the basket out of the hot, bubbling oil and removed the fries, dumping them inside of a tray lined with wax paper. Next, he sprinkled Lawry's seasoning salt on them.

Once Jayvon finished preparing the double cheeseburger combo, he put the lid on an XL diet Coca Cola, and loaded everything onto an orange food tray. He wiped the perspiration from his sweaty face again and lifted up the tray. As soon as he turned around he bumped into his boss Augustus and nearly spilled everything. Augustus was a fifty-seven-year-old, light-skinned black man with freckles on his face. He sported short graying curly hair and a graying beard. The old head was wearing a hairnet and a food stained apron over a white T-shirt. His hairy arms were nearly as big as the cartoon character Popeye.

"Damn, youngster, watch where you're going, shit," Augustus said with a wrinkled forehead. He'd just come from loading a couple boxes of meat inside of the walk-in freezer and had returned to the kitchen to work the cash register.

"My bad, OG," Jayvon told him.

Augustus glanced down at the double cheeseburger combo on the tray. Then he stole a glance at the old gold Timex watch on his wrist. "Double cheeseburger. No lettuce, grilled onions, tomatoes and extra Thousand Island dressing. Lemme guess, your best fucking buddy is here, ain't he?" He plucked one of the fries from out of the basket and tossed it in his mouth.

"Yep," Jayvon replied, nodding to one of the patrons.

Augustus looked in the direction he'd nodded and saw a thirty-something black man sitting at one of the tables. He was brown-skinned with a crop of dreadlocks that were nappy at their roots. He had them pulled back in a ponytail with a pink ribbon tied around them. The man had an unkempt beard and he wore flip-up, round lens eyeglasses/shades, like Dwayne Wayne in the *A Different World* television show. His attire was a worn black leather motorcycle jacket and army green cargo pants. The man sat a vase of beautiful red roses on the opposite side of the table, kissed the picture he had in his hand, and propped it up against it. He then went on carrying a conversation with the picture like it could respond back to him.

"That brother there is as nutty as squirrel shit," Augustus claimed, watching the man closely. "He eats here every day, same spot, same time talking to that picture of his wife."

"And?" Jayvon shrugged like, *What's the big deal?*

Augustus looked at him curling his upper lip. "*And* someone needs to have his crazy ass committed to Roosevelt Island along with the rest of the fucking quacks." He grabbed a towel and began wiping down the counter top.

"Man, lay off my guy. I fucks with him hard body," Jayvon told him. "Besides, yo' greedy ass has yet to ban him from eatin' here."

"You goddamn right, money talks and bullshit walks." Augustus replied.

Jayvon laughed and shook his head as he headed in the dreadlocks' direction. He watched as his head moved around like he was following something. Jayvon couldn't see what had his attention so he looked crazy as hell to him.

"Yo, old man, I'm taking my break after this," Jayvon told Augustus, but kept his eyes on dreadlocks.

"You spend more time on breaks than you do working in this muthafucka. Hell am I paying you for?" Augustus replied, twisting up his towel and creating a whip.

"Are you kidding me? With my paychecks, I'll be able to buy that spot I've been eyeing on Park Avenue in the next thirty, forty y—Ahhhh!" Jayvon hollered. Augustus had crept up behind him and lashed the back of his neck with the twisted towel. Holding the tray, Jayvon swung around and tried to kick him but he jumped back.

"I knew yo' ol' smart ass was gon' have something slick to say. That's why I snuck on over here," Augustus told him, as he flapped out the towel and laid it over his shoulder.

Jayvon laughed and rubbed the back of his stinging neck. "You and I are gonna box one day, old man."

Don't let these gray hairs fool you, youngster. Ol' Gus was a golden gloves champ in his day, check my footwork." Augustus danced around like a professional fighter, shadow boxing an imaginary opponent. The patrons laughed and giggled, cheering him on. "Trust me. This ain't what you want." He turned around and headed back inside of the kitchen.

Jayvon and Chyna had a fantastic relationship with Augustus. The old man acted as a protector and mentor to them when they were left wards of the streets. He had given Jayvon a gig at his burger joint, Augustus's World Famous Burgers and Milkshakes.

93

Although he didn't make that much, Jayvon's hustling weed on the side was enough to keep a roof over him and his brother's head, especially after their crib was ransacked and all of their father's drug money was stolen.

Jayvon sat the tray on the table before the dude with the dreadlocks and shook up with him. He had christened him Bag Man because he always kept a Crown Royal bag full of quarters. He used those same quarters to pay for everything he wanted and needed—even the double cheese burger combo he'd ordered that night. All that change was a pain in the ass to Augustus so Jayvon would take over at the register whenever Bag Man dined in. He reasoned Bag Man already had a hard life and he didn't want to add to it by giving him grief about the money he used to purchase his food. Besides, the two of them considered each other friends. They'd play chess at Central Park, run games of basketball, and shoot the shit over cheap booze from time to time.

"Bag Man, what up, G?" Jayvon greeted him.

"Ain't shit, just here finna have dinner with the wife," Bag Man replied. He then went back to looking at whatever had his attention. Jayvon looked from him to the picture he'd propped up against the vase of roses. It was a picture of his late wife, Valentina. Jayvon's forehead wrinkled as he searched for what had Bag Man's sole focus. He was surprised to see a fly zipping around as if he was taunting his friend. "Aren't you gonna say, hi, bitch?"

"Well, excuse me, *bitch.*" Jayvon hurled an insult right back. He and Bag Man talked harshly to each other like this all the time. This was how they showed each other love. "Pardon my language, Mrs. Harris. You're looking as beautiful as ever. How are—"

"Shhhhh." Bag Man hushed him, keeping his eyes on the fly. Jayvon scratched his temple trying to figure out what was the deal between Bag Man and the fly. He watched as Bag Man picked up his straw and removed its white paper wrapping. Tearing a smaller piece of the paper off it, he formed a wet ball out of it in his mouth, and brought the end of the straw to his lips. "You see his ass?" Jayvon nodded his answer. "Good. Here's your first lesson, take notes as you watch a master at work."

Jayvon made a face like *Whatever, nigga*, and folded his arms across his chest. Bag Man placed the end of the straw to his lips, slipped the spitball inside of his straw skillfully, and kept a keen eye on the fly. Jayvon's eyes jumped back and forth between Bag Man and the fly.

Bag Man blew into the end of the straw. The spitball rocketed out of the opposite side, and zipped through the air. It was en route to the fly as it was making a 360 degree turn. The spitball collided with the fly, launching it backwards and splattering it against the wall. Smothered in a glob of Bag Man's hot saliva, the fly slid down the wall and fell to the floor.

The patrons gave Bag Man a standing ovation as he stood up, bowing to his left and his right.

"Yo, Bag Man, that was fucking amazing. You've gotta teach me that one day." Jayvon shook up with him.

"Ain't shit. You know I'ma teach my main man," Bag Man replied, tossing a fry in his mouth and sitting back down.

Jayvon looked over his shoulder and a smile emerged. He saw Chrissy through the large windows of the establishment. She was chewing gum while standing on the corner with a duffle bag. By the way she was looking up and down the street, he could tell she was looking for her ride to drive up at any moment.

"Excuse me, main man, but I'ma go holla at this fine young lady across the street," Jayvon informed him while keeping his eyes on Chrissy.

"Go ahead, youngin', I'm hungry as a hostage," Bag Man claimed with a mouthful of food, stuffing his face.

"If you don't mind, I'ma need them big ass glasses of yours to make sure a brother is right," Jayvon said. When Bag Man looked his way, he fixed his hair and straightened the wrinkles in his clothes. "Okay, how do I look?" He struck several poses.

Bag Man looked him up and down before answering, "Well, you know what they say, right?"

"Nah, what do they say?" Jayvon asked curiously.

"No matter how you dress up a turd, it's still a piece of shit,"Bag Man replied and went back to eating his meal.

"Man, I should…" Jayvon threw a few phantom punches at Bag Man and playfully shoved him.

Jayvon removed his apron and disappeared into the back. He returned, slipping a hoodie over his head and adjusting it. He walked past the kitchen and Augustus stuck his head out of the entrance.

"Fifteen minutes, young blood. I'll be keeping time," Augustus called after him, tapping his finger against the face of his watch.

Bag Man drew one of the roses from out of the vase his wife's picture was propped against and held it out to Jayvon. Jayvon plucked the rose out of Bag Man's hand, touched fists with him and walked out of the door.

CHAPTER FIFTEEN

Jayvon looked both ways before jogging across the street. The wind blew, disturbing Chrissy's flat-ironed hair and clothes. She tucked her hair behind her ear and smiled as Jayvon approached her. He was holding something behind his back but she didn't have an inkling of what it was.

"What's up, Doll?" Jayvon smiled, presenting her with the rose.

"Hey, handsome, how have you been?" Chrissy blushed as she received the rose and inhaled its scent. She had never been with anyone that treated her like Jayvon did. He always made her feel like she was the only girl in the world that mattered to him.

"Ain't shit, taking a break from the plantation." Jayvon replied, taking a cigarette from his wrinkled pack of Newports and lighting it up. Unbeknownst to him, Chrissy was taking in his appearance from head to toe, and it was making her lady parts tingle. Jayvon had runway model good-looks and a fit muscular body. His eyes were hazel-brown and his skin was the color of Spanish coffee beans. He had a five o'clock shadow, and new growth caused his short wavy hair to form into curls. He was an inch under six-feet, weighed approximately 175-pounds, and at twenty years of age he was exactly one year older than the love of his life.

"Thanks for the rose." Chrissy said, unzipping the duffle bag and placing the rose inside of it.

Jayvon blew out a cloud of smoke. "Don't mention it. You know you got it like that."

"Oh, really?"

"Yep."

"Well, gemme a kiss then."

Jayvon kissed Chrissy twice but she held him and kissed him three more times. When she pulled back they were both smiling.

"Excuse me, Ms. Thang, but *a* mean's one. Not five, greedy ass."

Chrissy kissed him once more. "Now that's greedy."

Jayvon's brows furrowed, noticing something about Chrissy. "You look tired, Doll, long night?"

Chrissy, still holding the duffle bag, yawned and stretched her arms. "Excuse me. But yeah, they worked yo' girl like a slave tonight. I can't wait 'til this nigga Purp gets here so I can get back home. I'ma take a nice, hot, bath, sip a little white wine and listening to Ms. Scott until I fall a—"

Chrissy's words died in her throat when a masked man ran up and pointed a gun in her face.

"Come up off that bag, bitch!" the masked man ordered. Scared, Chrissy handed the duffle bags over. The masked man slipped the duffle bag's strap over his shoulder, pointed his stick at Jayvon and slowly backed away. He made note of his scowl and clenched jaws. "Yo, son, I suggest you fall back, 'less you're made of kevlar or some shit." The masked man took off running towards a midnight blue Chrysler 300.

"Oh, my God! All the money I made tonight is in those bags!" Chrissy cried.

Jayvon threw his cigarette and chased after the masked man that stole Chrissy's duffle bag. For as fast as the jack boy was Jayvon was that much faster.

Jayvon swept the heel of the man's sneaker from under him while he was in motion. The masked man lost the duffle bag as his face slammed into the sidewalk. The impact sent his gun flying from under him. Jayvon threw up his fists. The jack boy stood up on his hands and knees. He scanned the ground for his gun but he couldn't find it.

"Get up! Get cho bitch ass up." Jayvon spat, kicking him in his ass while he struggled to get up. The jack boy snatched off his ski mask, exposing his busted nose and bloody mouth. He angrily slung his ski mask aside, drew a butterfly knife, and triggered its blade. It was so shiny it glowed in the night for a moment.

"I'm gonna teach you to stay outta business that doesn't concern you, homeboy." The jack boy tried to take a swipe at Jayvon, but he missed him. He tried thrusting the knife into Jayvon's abdomen, but he gracefully avoided it. Expertly, Jayvon locked his arms around the man's arm and popped it. He hollered in agony and dropped the butterfly knife. The man's arm dangled limply at his side. His eyes jumped from Jayvon to the knife he'd dropped on the sidewalk. Jayvon smirked knowing the jack boy thought he could take him with the knife. He was confident he could whip his ass with or without it, so he kicked it over to him. The man picked up the knife and smiled wickedly.

"You've gotta be one of the stupidest muthafuckaz to have ever woken up this morning!" The man said, swinging the knife wildly and then jabbing it at Jayvon's face. Jayvon slipped aside, locked his arms around the man's other arm and popped it as well. Teary eyed, the man threw his head back screaming.

Seeing the man with two broken arms dangling at his sides amused Jayvon. He nearly laughed when he tried kicking him. Jayvon moved from side to side, swatting his feet away. He countered by kicking him in his balls, which made him bend at the waist. Jayvob followed up with an uppercut that dropped him on his back.

"Chump!" Jayvon spat on his face and held up the duffle bag for Chrissy to see. She smiled and threw her fist up cheerfully. The celebration was short-lived when Jayvon felt a cold gun against the back of his neck. The tiny hairs on his arms stood up and his heart raced.

"I think you got something that belongs to me." A masked gunman said, cocking the hammer back of his piece. He was the getaway driver of the midnight blue Chrysler 300. He hopped out with his pole the moment he saw his man go down.

"It's all yours, my nigga." Jayvon passed him the duffel bag without turning around.

The masked gunman slipped the strap of the duffle bag over his shoulders and helped his crime partner to his feet. Together, they made hurried footsteps towards the getaway car. They'd cleared a third of the block before a dark figure flew out of the shadows like a frightened pigeon. Swiftly, it struck the man with the broken arms in the forehead, torso and swept him off his feet. The dark figure, who was actually Bag Man, knocked the gun out of the masked gunman's hand. Using his bamboo stick, Bag Man jabbed the gunman in the throat, chest, stomach and balls. The masked gunman, dropping the duffle bag in the process, grabbed each individual area where he'd been attacked. Before he could mount a defense, Bag Man did a spinning heel kick that sent the ground flying up against the side of his face.

As both of the men laid defeated, Bag Man picked up the duffle bag and tossed it to Chrissy. She thanked him and checked the duffle bag. All the money she'd earned that night was still there. She smiled and unzipped the duffle bag back up.

"Y'all okay out here?" Augustus asked as he hurried across the street with his hand on his holstered. He'd caught the last of what occurred outside and had came out to lay some niggas down in the name of Jayvon.

"We're a'ight, OG. Look at chu coming out here ready to slump something on the behalf of your boy. That's love." Jayvon grinned, patting him on his shoulder.

Augustus smacked his hand off his shoulder. "Negro, please, I'm just looking out for my best interest. Where else am I going to find someone to work for the wages I pay?"

Jayvon laughed and threw playful punches at Augustus. He threw some back and they laughed about it. Chrissy kissed all of them on their cheek and thanked them as a collective.

"Come on, Bag Man, there's a root beer float on the house waiting for ya." Augustus said, heading back to his place of business with Bag Man on his heels.

"Good looking out, Bag Man." Jayvon yelled across the street to Bag Man. He threw up his hand as he disappeared through the door of Augustus's establishment.

Jayvon looked at the spot where Bag Man had laid out the two jack boys and they had vanished. His brows furrowed seeing their Chrysler 300 speeding down the street.

Jayvon located the guns they'd used in the botched robbery and deposited them in the gutter. Thereafter, an ox-blood red Rolls Royce Phantom Limousine on 22-inch gold Forgiato Trimestre rims drove up, stealing Jayvon and Chrissy's attention. The luxury whip's music was so loud its body trembled with the song's bass. The back passenger window descended and revealed Bartise. The forty-three-year-old, stocky drug lord was wearing an Armani suit the same color as his Rolls Royce. His shoulder length dreadlocks were braided into plaits and his five o'clock shadow was trimmed to perfection.

Bartise was just about to say something to Chrissy when he realized the music was entirely too loud for her to hear him. His face balled up with agitation as he looked up front at the chauffeur.

"Purp, do me a favor and turn that bullshit down, will ya?" Bartise hollered up front. A second later the volume was turned down to a little above a whisper. "Thank you. Chrissy, come around to the other side and hop in."

Chrissy kissed Jayvon and gave him a hug. They exchanged *I love yous* and she ran around to the other side of the limousine and hopped inside.

"What's up, nigga? Everything good?" Bartise asked Jayvon, looking him up and down, placing his pistol in his lap. Jayvon was mad dogging Bartise with his hands in the pockets of his hoodie. Bartise knew homie wasn't a fan of his considering he had his bitch under lock and key, so he had to be ready for a potential conflict.

Chrissy panicked when she locked eyes on the gun Bartise placed in his lap. She knew Jayvon wouldn't back down even with his life in jeopardy.

"Actually, everything isn't all good." Chrissy interjected, drawing Bartise's attention. "Two stickup kids tried to take the money I earned tonight. If it wasn't for my man and his friends, I would have come up short, maybe even killed."

"Is that right, Jayvon?" Bartise asked Jayvon.

"I just told y—"

Bartise snapped. "Bitch, is your name Jayvon?"

Jayvon squared his jaws and balled his fists. He was about to wild out on Bartise until Chrissy turned her pleading eyes on him. He closed his eyes and took a deep breath to put his emotions in check.

Jayvon nodded. "Yeah. We held it down."

"Chris is workin' towards paying off her debt, so technically she's still mine. With that being said, I'd like to compensate you for protecting my investment." Bartise shoved his piece inside the holster in his suit. He pulled out a wad of blue face one hundred dollar bills, removed the gold money clip, and licked his thumb. "How does five hundred dollars sound? Should that do it?"

"Nah, I can't take that. It's my job to protect my lady." Jayvon threw his hand up.

"You one of those honorable negroes, huh? I feel you black man." Bartise placed his money clip back on his wad and pocketed it. "Purp, mush."

The Rolls Royce limousine drove away, leaving Jayvon standing on the sidewalk. He walked out into the street and watched the backlights of the $455,000 whip until they vanished into the night. A sharp whistle drew Jayvon's attention to the entrance of Augustus's burger spot. The old man hung halfway out of the door, motioning him over.

"Aye, lover boy, your break was over ten minutes ago! I need you in here pronto, move your ass!" Augustus told him. Jayvon grinned and shook his head, thinking of how unapologetically rude Augustus was. He then looked both ways and jogged across the street.

***

The Rolls Royce Phantom limousine was deathly quiet as Bartise and Chrissy rode in the backseat. Chrissy sat beside him with her duffle bag on the side of her. She looked around nervously fidgeting with her fingers. Bartise, who didn't appear to be paying her any attention, took the liberty to pour himself a glass of ridiculously expensive Cognac. He stuck the cork back inside the neck of the bottle and set it aside. He took a sip of the dark liquor, savored the taste and licked his lips.

"This my trap?" Bartise asked, pulling Chrissy's duffle bag close.

"Yeah. That's you." Chrissy assured him.

Bartise unzipped the duffle bag and peered inside. He smiled and licked his top row of teeth, pleased by all the dead faces. Taking another sip of alcohol, he sat his glass inside of the holder and brought the duffle bag to his nose. He closed his eyes and inhaled deeply. A smile spread across lips and he threw his head back. He sat the duffle bag in his lap and pulled out two handfuls of cash.

"There ain't shit like new money." Bartise said to no one in particular, enjoying the feeling of every bill in his hands.

"New pussy." Hamza responded from the opposite side of the limousine. The sound of his voice startled Chrissy. She was so focused on Bartise that she neglected the presence of the six-foot-three Arabic man. He wore a checkered red and white Shemagh head to neck length scarf with a Egal Headband around it. His hands boasted calluses, old scars and teeth marks from the men he'd fought. Hamza was Bartise's one and only fighter in the underground fighting network.

"Youz a damn fool, Sandman. I'd pass up a piece of ass for a handful of cash anytime." Bartise replied, stuffing the money back inside the duffle bag. He frowned when he saw the rose Chrissy had stashed there before the botched robbery attempt. He picked it up and held it before her eyes. "Fuck is this?"

Chrissy snatched the rose out of his hand. "It's a rose. My man gave it to me."

"That figures. Oh, sucka for love ass nigga." Bartise said under his breath, zipping up the duffle bag and sitting it beside him. He locked eyes with Hamza who nodded towards Chrissy. "Oh, yeah, Chrissy, I want chu to take care of Hamza once we get back. The Arabian Prince here, walked away victorious tonight. Nigga brought yo' boy in a wholllle lotta cash." Bartise refilled his glass with Cognac and took a sip. Chrissy stared out of the passenger window, watching the streets whip past her. Bartise was steadily talking to her but she'd closed her eyes and imagined herself in a happier place at a happier time. It wasn't until Bartise squeezed her thigh that she snapped back to the present.

"Ow. I don't fuck around like that anymore, Bartise." Chrissy replied.

"I'll tell you what, shorty, take care of my man tonight, and I'll knock fifty-grand off yo' debt. How does that sound?" Bartise asked.

"I'm in a loving, committed relationship. I gave that lifestyle up as soon as Jayvon and I became an item." Chrissy told him. "I'ma lotta things but I'm not disloyal."

Bartise looked at Hamza and said, "Aye, bruh, I tried."

Fuck, Hamza thought, scrolling through the I.G. pages of half-naked bitchez twerking and popping their pussies.

Chrissy closed her eyes and inhaled the scent of the rose. Staring out of the passenger window, she saw her and Jayvon standing at the altar. It was their wedding and everyone and their baby daddy was present. Chyna and Bag Man were the best men while Augustus was to give her away. It was a beautiful, sunny day with bees swarming and birds chirping, soaring through the air.

Closing her eyes, Chrissy leaned against the window and inhaled the scent of the rose again. She fell asleep with a smile on her face, dreaming of her and Jayvon's honeymoon.

CHAPTER SIXTEEN

It was one o'clock in the afternoon and the sun was beaming. It was as hot as teenage hood rat pussy but that didn't stop the neighborhood kids from horsing around, residences from tending to their lawns, or the dopeboys from hustling. Bag Man stood in front of Augustus's burger spot practicing with his katana which doubled as a bamboo stick. He envisioned himself slicing through the limbs of his enemies and listening to their horrified screams. Their agony aroused him, pushing him to go harder, faster and spill what appeared to be buckets of sweat.

Bag Man leaped up, swung his katana around in a 360-degree turn and landed in a kneeling position. He held his position with his katana at his back breathing heavily. Bag Mag wiped the sweat dripping from his brow, sheathed his katana inside the second half of his bamboo stick and stashed it inside of his shopping cart full of goods. He drew an old dingy bandana from his back pocket and wiped his face and chest down. As he slipped a Jamaican tank top over his head, he saw Jayvon walking up the block kicking an empty soda can. Bag Man could tell something was bothering him, and he was curious as to what it was.

"Boy, if you aren't the saddest, ugliest fucking bitch I've ever seen in my life." Bag Man addressed Jayvon as he approached. "What happened, sweetheart? Your boyfriend broke up witchu?"

Jayvon looked up wearing the faintest trace of a smile. "Man, fuck you."

"Naw. Seriously, what's going on? And don't lie either, or I'll kick yo' ass."

Jayvon took a breath before telling Bag Man him and Chrissy's money situation. Bag Man, recalling how Jayvon handled those stickup kids the other night, gave his situation some thought. He knew a way Jayvon could get some money but he wasn't sure if he'd be down with it or not.

"What if I were to tell you I gotta way for you to come up with some of that bread?"

"I'd say I'm all ears."

"Good. Step into my office." Bag Man hung his arm around Jayvon's shoulders and walked him over to his shopping cart. He told him about an underground fighting tournament that was to take place Friday night. The winner stood to win big, really big—$100,000 dollars, exactly. "I figure we take all that we have and put it on you to win. As long as you come out on top, we stand to walk away with one hell of a check."

My nigga, youa fuckin' bum! Hell you get money from? Son, musta saved up hella cans and bottles and recycled them shits, Jayvon thought. He didn't have the heart to ask Bag Man where he'd gotten money for fear he'd offend him.

"I'm with it." Jayvon replied, punching his fist into his palm. "I don't care if I gotta crush two, three hunnit niggaz to get that bread up. I'ma do it. I gotta see to it my queen comes home."

"You're goddamn right you do. And I'ma throw inna few dollars of my own to see to it." A voice came from behind Bag Man and Jayvon. When they turned around was Augustus standing at the door of his business. He was wearing a food stained apron and a rag over his shoulder. He'd been listening in on the conversation all along.

"You mean that, unc?" Jayvon asked as he approached him.

"Sho' ya right." Augustus replied, shaking up with him and embracing.

***

Bag Man invited Jayvon to his place after he'd gotten off work. Jayvon was expecting a tent in some garbage-filled, piss smelling alley on his way over to his friend's home, but he got the surprise of a life-time when he finally laid eyes on his crib. Bag Man lived inside the basement of an old Puerto Rican couple's house. The place had wall-to-wall black carpet, charcoal-gray painted walls, light-gray suede couches and black & white portraits of some of the world's greatest fighters on the walls. Although Jayvon was captivated by the framed photographs, the mural on the other side of the basement really held his attention. It was dedicated to Bag Man's late-wife, Valentina. There was one large portrait at the top, center of the mantel surrounded by several small others, among them were tall and short candles. There were also items that he'd collected over the years they'd been in a relationship and married. A locket, a promise ring, ticket stubs from the first movie they'd seen together, souvenirs from every country they visited, etc.

"This is, uh, nice place you've got here." Jayvon said, taking in the scenery. He took the cold soda Bag

Man had given him when he returned from the small kitchen area.

"Don't be so obvious, bitch, you thought my lil' spot was gon' be some hole-in-the-wall, with roaches and rats runnin' around, huh?" Bag Man smirked and cracked open a cold beverage of his own.

A surprised look crossed Jayvon's face. He hadn't known better he would have thought Bag Man had read his mind. "Uh, nah, naw, hell naw. You know what they say, never judge a book by its cover." He took a drink of soda.

Bag Man twisted his lips and looked at him sideways. "Unh huh, lie to momma but tell daddy the truth."

"Yeah. Whatever the fuck that means."

Bag Man removed his eyeglasses and stripped down to his tank top. He motioned for Jayvon to follow him as he walked towards his bedroom door. "I wanna show you somethin'."

Bag Man opened the bedroom door and flipped on the light switch. Jayvon's forehead and nose scrunched when he stepped in beside him. There wasn't a bed, furniture, or television-set occupying the space. Instead, there were buckets stacked upon buckets of bird feed.

Jayvon stepped further inside and took a closer look. He wanted to make sure there was only bird feed occupying the bedroom.

"My G, if all you've got to eat in this bitch is bird feed then you're gon' be one hungry ass. Check it, you my man, I can't let chu go out like that. I gotta couple dollars. Let's head down to the bodega and get chu—"

112

Smack!

Bag Man smacked Jayvon upside the back of his head. "Stupid bitch." He said under his breath, shaking his head and walking towards the stacked buckets of bird feed.

"Aye, man, that shit hurt." Jayvon frowned, rubbing the back of his head.

"Well, it's not supposed to feel good, muthafucka." Bag Man sat his soda down on top of one of the buckets and began to peel off one of their lids.

"I should kick yo' ass."

"Yeah. Yeah. Yeah. Bring yo' ass over here." Bag Man removed the lid and sat it aside. He then removed the lids of others.

Jayvon looked inside each of the buckets. They were all filled to the very top with quarters. Jayvon dipped his hands inside one of the buckets. He lifted a pile of coins and allowed them to run between his fingers.

"Yo, all of these buckets are full of quarters?"

"Yep. I made all of this by workin'. I never took a handout or panhandled. A nigga got too much pride and ambition for that shit. You smell me?"

Jayvon nodded understandingly. "What chu savin' up these coins for? A rainy day?"

"Nah. This here is every last penny I have in the world." Bag Man assured him. "I'm takin' it all and placin' it on you."

"Me?" Jayvon's eyes became the size of golf balls. "You've got that much faith in the kid, that you're willin' to put your life savings onna line?" Bag Man folded his arms across his chest and nodded

113

assuringly. "That's a hell of a lot of pressure to put on ya boy's shoulders. I'll not only have the weight of winnin' this bread for my girl but the weight of knowin' all yo' loot will be ridin' on me, too."

"Exactly," Bag Man placed his hand on his shoulder and looked him in his eyes. "That pressure is gonna bring the determination outta you. That hunger for the win will catapult you to victory. I know you can do it, bitch, 'cause I see it in you. You've got the same look in your eyes as the Ex-Man."

"Wait, nigga, you knew the Ex-Man?"

"Not only did I know him, I trained 'em."

"You shittin' me, bruh?"

"Not at all," Bag Man took a drink from his soda.

Ex-Man was somewhat of a legend in the underground fighting circuit. It was said he bowled over his competition in every match. There was absolutely no one that could defeat him. It was said this was because of his dedication to training and his determination to win. What every fan and hater of his didn't know was he was fighting for a cause. A very unique cause that no one would find out about until years later.

"What the hell happened to homie? After that match with Napalm it was like he vanished from the face of the earth."

"Hell, if I know." Bag Man replied, finishing his soda and belching. "He gave me my cut of the winnings that same night and disappeared. Brother cut off his house phone and his cellphone. I went by his crib and he had moved out."

"You didn't try to dig deeper to find 'em?"

"Nah. If a man goes through alla that to disappear, I'm for certain he doesn't want to be found, and I for one am gonna respect his wishes."

Jayvon stared ahead vacantly nodding his head.

"Say, bitch, let's say we cash these coins in for dollars. Then I'll show you some of the moves I taught the Ex-Man?"

Jayvon downed the rest of his soda and sat it on one of the buckets. "A'ight. I'm with that."

Jayvon and Bag Man loaded all of the buckets into the back of his landlord's pickup truck. They unloaded the haul at a nearby Bank of America. In all, Bag Man walked away with a sum of $90, 500. 50. When they made it back to Bag Man's place, he stashed the loot in a secret hiding space in his bathroom's ceiling. Then he showed Jayvon a few moves he'd taught Ex-Man. Two hours later, Jayvon was lying on the floor sweaty and trying to catch his breath. Bag Man returned from the kitchen with two bottled waters, drying his forehead with a white towel that was lying over his right shoulder.

"Heads up, youngin'." Bag Man tossed Jayvon one of the bottled waters as he sat up on the floor. He thanked him as he twisted off the cap and guzzled half of it. "We've gotta few days before the fight. I'm thinkin' we go hard with the trainin' with the lil' time we have. Whatta ya say?"

"I'm down with whatever's gonna increase my chances of winnin' this thing." Jayvon finished his water and sat it on the coffee table. He got dressed, shook up with Bag Man, and made arrangements for them to train tomorrow.

Tranay Adams

CHAPTER SEVENTEEN

Fight night

The rooftop of the club was packed with spectators cheering for their favorite fighter to win. The repugnant odor of sweat and blood lingered in the air. The sound of bare knuckles, elbows, knees and feet striking flesh and groans of pain infected the night's air.

"Come on, bro, whip his ass!" Chyna called out to Jayvon.

"You got this, young blood, bring it home!" Angustus called out from beside Chyna.

"Yeah, fuck 'em up, bitch! You got this!" Bag Man said with a cheek full of food. He was eating Buffalo wings from a black styrofoam container and taking the occasional swig of a beer. "Goddamn, these wings are good as a muthafucka." He sucked the sauce off his fingers.

Purp, who was gnawing on a toothpick, glanced at Bartise whose eyes were glued on the fight. Though he didn't give a rat's ass who won, he knew Bartise did, he'd seen the wealthy fuck drop $1,000,000 on Hamza to win. Bartise thought Jayvon was going to be an easy win but the kid was proving to be a worthy opponent.

"What's got cho dick inna zippa, kid?" Purp asked Bartise. He knew why the kingpin was worried but he wanted to hear it from him.

"Do me a favor, Purp." Bartise said. Purp threw his head back like *What's up?* But before he could answer Hamza crashed into him with a face that looked like bloody hamburger meat. Bartise grabbed hold of him from behind and spoke into his ear. "Either you beat this lil' shit, or I'ma have Purp and Stutter-Box toss yo' camel ridin' ass off the Brooklyn Bridge, ya hear?" Hamza nodded and spat out a bloody tooth. "Good. Now, get cho big ass back in there!" He shoved him back into the fight.

"About that favor?" Purp asked, keeping a close eye on the brawl.

Bartise brushed off his shoulders and sleeves. He fogged his diamond pinky ring and wiped it on his slacks. "Yeah. Shut the fuck up."

Purp smirked and continued to watch the fight.

That's it, baby, whip his muthafuckin' ass! Show homeboy how y'all give it up in Brooklyn, Chrissy thought. She kept what she was thinking to herself for fear of Bartise's reaction. She knew he had some serious paper on the line and the wrong thing said could lead to him putting a serious hurting on her.

Chrissy was dressed to impress that night on the rooftop. She had on a black Cleopatra wig that hung past her shoulders and her face was beat like an Egyptian goddess, with a splash of glitter. She wore a fur coat with a lion's head on its right shoulder over a golden-brown thermal dress that hugged every one of her curves. What really set her ensemble off was the diamond tennis necklace with Bartise's name in cursive. It was flooded with VVs diamonds. Bartise wanted niggaz to know that shorty belonged to him and the necklace was perfect for that.

Feeling a pair of eyes on him, Bartise looked over his shoulder to find Bag Man watching him. Bag Man looked away and pretended he hadn't been paying the kingpin any mind. Bartise couldn't put his finger on it but there was something about his eyes that made him feel like he knew him. If he was to cut his hair and shave off his facial hair he'd probably recall where he knew him from. Then again, what good would knowing him given his current circumstances? He looked at Bag Man as an old bum with no money or worldly connections so he didn't stand to gain anything by associating with him.

The sudden roar of the audience drew Bartise's attention back to the brawl. Hamza was swinging weakly at Jayvon who was ducking his advances and giving him haymakers. The devastating blows whipped Hamza's battered head from left to right. He took a step backwards with each and every punch Jayvon connected. Hamza kept swinging but each one came slower and slower. His eyes were rolling around in his head and he was bleeding from his mouth badly. Jayvon was on the verge of passing out from exhaustion but he had to push forward if he was going to steal the victory. Jayvon attacked Hamza vengefully. He laid into him hard and fast until he finally fell to his defeat. Jayvon nearly fell with him, but luckily Chyna caught him before he could greet the ground. Augustus and Bag Man rushed in behind Chyna to tend to Jayvon. Though Chrissy desperately wanted to follow behind them, the death-stare Bartise gave her held her firmly in place. The referee, a Japanese youth with spiky blonde hair, lifted Jayvon's hand in the air and declared him the victor. Most of the audience was disappointed having betted on Hamza, but those who had their money riding on Jayvon were joyous.

Bartise's stomach dropped like he was on a roller coaster when saw Hamza fall in what seemed like slow-motion over and over again. He closed his eyes and balled his fists. Bartise meditated for a minute, taking a breath and trying to calm himself down. Peeling his eyes open, he motioned Purp over and whispered something into his ear. Purp nodded his understanding of the task he'd been given. He whispered to Stutter-Box the orders he'd been given as they walked towards Hamza.

Chyna and Bag Man helped Jayvon up. He locked eyes with Chrissy and they exchanged smiles. She blew him a kiss on the low and he winked at her. He then mouthed to her "I'm coming for you, baby", which meant he was going to buy her back from Bartise. She touched her heart with both hands and nodded back.

"You did good out there, kid. We won big. I mean, really big." Bag Man told him. "Here, have a drink." He extended his beer to Jayvon.

Augustus, holding a silver flask, bumped Bag Man out of the way. "That domesticated crap is not gonna do jack shit for 'em. Here, junior, try this. It's my great, great grandfather's very own concoction. Old nigga taught the nigga that taught that white nigga Jack Daniel's, how to make his whiskey." Jayvon drank from the flask and made a bitter face. "Yeah, it hits like a round from an old Confederate cannon, but it does its job."

"Good looking out, unc." Jayvon said before taking another drink. He caught Bartise giving him a look like he wanted to holler at him. "Look, I think homeboy wants to talk, why don't you and baby bro collect our winnings while we rap."

Chyna and Augustus mad dogged Bartise as he and Chrissy made their way over in their direction.

"You sure, bro? Son, giving me hella bad vibes." Chyna told Jayvon without taking his eyes off Bartise.

"I'm with the youngster," Augustus added, keeping his eyes on Bartise also.

"Y'all don't sweat it, the champ is in good hands." Bag Man downed what was left of his beer, belched and chucked the empty bottle aside. He had a watchful eye on Bartise too. The kingpin had a bad aura around him and he trusted him as far as he could see him.

"A'ight then. Let's go, unc." Chyna said, taking his brother's arm from around his shoulders. Augustus did the same and they made their way towards the rooftop's door.

The spectators who had betted on Jayvon to win gave him his props and shook up with him. With their women in tow, they then made their way to the rooftop door so they could collect their winnings downstairs in the club.

"Uh, what the, what the hell happened?" Hamza asked, with each of his arms over Purp and Stutter-Box's shoulders. He was bloody and sweaty, leaving a slippery trail behind him.

"What happened? What happened is you gotcho muthafuckin' ass whooped." Purp told him.

"Yep. And that—and that nigga Bartise ma—ma—mad as a mudda—muddafucka, too." Stutter-Box added his two cents.

"I honestly don't give a shit." Hamza winced. "I think I'm bleeding internally, and my ribs are broken. I may have a concussion, too."

"Don't worry, Sandman, we're gonna get chu to a hospital so they can fix you up real nice." Purp assured him before they disappeared through the rooftop's door.

"I must say, my nigga, I'm in complete awe of your performance. You and my boy Hamza put on one hell of a show." Bartise smiled, showcasing his beautiful white teeth.

"Appreciate the love." Jayvon replied, touching his fist to his chest. He spat blood on the rooftop and glanced at Bag Man who was slipping his glasses/shades over his eyes. It was like he was trying to avoid being recognized by Bartise. Though Jayvon thought this was strange, he knew now wasn't the time to bring it up so he decided to holler at Bag Man about it later.

"Listen, there isn't any other way for me to say this, so I'ma just come out and say it." Bartise told him. "I want chu to come fight for me. You agree, I'll give you your bitch back—" Jayvon looked at him sideways and he corrected himself. "Excuse me. I'll give you your queen back, and you get to keep whatever loot you raised to pay for her return. How does that float yo' boat, champ?"

"Thanks but I'll have to respectfully decline. Loyalty means everything to me so I could never turn my back on my team." Jayvon replied.

"I wouldn't want you to. Hell would I want to fuck up wutchu and yours got goin'? Clearly, it's a winning formula." Bartise grinned. "Look, we'll keep you and your team together. I'll throw in a big ass mansion for all of y'all to live in, your own ride of your choosing, no matter the cost. You know what? Fuck it! My number one can't be driving himself around, we're gonna get chu yo' own Rolls Royce Phantom—chauffeur driven. I'll even toss inna $200,000 dollar sign on bonus. All you've gotta do is sign a—"

"Yo, my man, all of that sounds good, but if it's all the same to you. I'd like to keep the same deal we've always had." Jayvon cut him short. "I'll have that bag for you tomorrow night, say around ten o'clock. You just lemme know where you want me to make the drop."

Bartise was so hot he could feel the blood flowing through his veins boiling. His face attempted to scrunch in anger but he fought it back. He managed a smile and told Jayvon where the drop was to take place.

"Again, you put on one hell of a show." Bartise smiled and outstretched his hand. Jayvon looked down at his hand, then to Bag Man who shrugged, then back at Bartise, shaking his hand. "My nigga."

Bartise patted Jayvon on his shoulder and walked away with Chrissy on his arm. Jayvon brushed his shoulder off. He and Chrissy locked eyes once again. They mouthed "I love you". Then he made a vow to get her back. She nodded, understanding his stance on them being back together again.

Four men wearing surgical masks, latex gloves and navy blue jumpsuits came up through the rooftop's door. They had black industrial size garbage bags, cleaning supplies and equipment. They walked past Bartise and Chrissy who were heading out of the door.

"Yo, you know homeboy or something?" A frowning Jayvon asked Bag Man about Bartise.

Bag Man's face balled up. "Who? Bartise? Naw, I don't know dude. I think I've seen 'em around before but I don't personally know 'em."

Bag Man's cellphone chimed with a text message. He pulled it out and took a look at the display. "Yo, this is Chyna. Him and Gus are down in the truck. They've got the money so let's roll."

Something tells me notta believe this nigga and I don't know why. I'ma just focus on gettin' Chris back then I'll find out the real deal with him and Bartise, Jayvon thought, accepting Bag Man's bamboo stick for balance and allowing him to stretch his arm around his shoulders.

CHAPTER EIGHTEEN

Cars whipped up and down the Brooklyn Bridge nearly striking a masked Purp and Stutter Box as they removed a struggling Hamza from their truck. Hamza screamed, yanking and pulling his arms and legs. He pleaded with them to spare his life but it fell on deaf ears. When he looked over his shoulder and saw what they planned to do with him he really went crazy.

"Oh, Allah, Allah, please, have mercy! I can't die. I can't die like this!" Hamza screamed with eyes as big as pool balls. He was so terrified he pissed his pants. It wasn't so much as the fall that scared him but the water. He didn't know how to swim so if the fall didn't kill him the water most definitely would.

"Stop—stop—stop cryin' like a—like a—lil' girl, son! Take yo'—take yo' medicine like a—like a ma—man!" Stutter-Box told Hamza while carrying him over to the edge of the bridge.

"Yeah. You heard my dawg, take—take—take yo' medicine like a—like a—ma—man!" Purp mocked Stutter-Box and laughed hardily. "Okay, Stutter-Box, you stuttering fuck, we're gonna rock this dick back and forth. Then on the count of three we're gonna toss 'em over."

"Then we'll find—find out—if—if shit can—if shit can float." Stutter- Box and Purp laughed heartily.

"Okay. Now one…two…three!" Purp called out.

"Noooooooo!" Hamza screamed as he was released from Purp and Stutter-Box's hands.

Purp and Stutter-Box looked over the bridge at Hamza in freefall. He flailed his arms and legs wildly. The surface of the water seemed to be coming up at him fast.

Purp didn't bother to watch Hamza fall the rest of the way. He nudged Stutter-Box and they walked back towards the van. "Come on, Stutter-Box, let's get outta here."

There was a big, loud splash below but they didn't pay it any mind. They piled back up inside of the van, merged back into traffic and sped up the bridge.

***

Augustus drove through the city with Bag Man sitting in the front passenger seat. Augustus sang along to Curtis Mayfield's *Ghetto Child* playing from the stereo. Bag Man focused his attention out of the window while gripping a sawed off shotgun. In the backseat, Chyna sat beside Jayvon. They both had their sticks in their laps. Everyone was holding on the account that they were riding with a big bag they knew the wolves would love to get their hands on. Chyna turned his attention from the window he was staring out of and looked at his brother's hands. They were bruised and busted but minutes ago they were stained with Hamza's blood. Chyna's mind went back and forth between seeing his brother's hands bloody, to seeing them how they were now. Suddenly, his eyebrows rose as something within his mind clicked like the hammer of a loaded revolver.

"That's it! That's gonna be your fight name." Chyna said excitedly.

"What the hell is he rambling about back there, youngster?" Augustus asked, turning the stereo down.

"We've been tryna come up with a name for me to fight under." Jayvon replied.

"Well, spit it out lil' nigga, got me in suspense and shit." Bag Man chimed in.

"Bloody Knuckles, son. On the account of you beatin' the dog shit outta dude back there." Chyna told him, anxiously waiting for his response.

Jayvon thought about it as he massaged his chin. He then nodded in agreement as a smirk graced his lips. "Yeah, Mighty Mouse, I fucks with that. I fucks with that heavy."

"I like it," Bag Man nodded his approval.

"Not bad, kid. It's a hell of a lot better than Killa Jay." Augustus added.

"Yeah. I don't know what the hell he was thinking when he came up with that one." Bag Man shook his head.

"Son, fuck the both of you old niggaz." Jayvon laughed.

The next night

Jayvon walked back and forth across the floor eagerly waiting to hear the amount of cash they'd gotten up. Bag Man and Augustus sat at the living room table counting dead presidents and crunching numbers. They needed at least eighty more grand to buy Chrissy back from Bartise. Jayvon had spoken with Chrissy on the jack last night. They had a very emotional conversation. Being locked up in Bartise's mansion for so long was starting to get the best of her. Her breaking down sobbing touched him. It was then he promised her he was going to get her back tomorrow night. He gave her his word, and if he had to he'd die trying to keep it.

"Fuck it! I'm gettin' that money for my shorty tonight," Jayvon claimed, picking up his stick from the table and cocking it. "Y'all niggaz gon' make this move with me?"

"And just what the fuck do you plan on doing with that, young blood?" Augustus asked, scratching his beard with the hand that held his cigar.

"I'm goin' all out for mine. Every dope boy in the city comin' up short 'til I collect what I need to get my baby back." Jayvon swore before slipping his hoodie over his head and sticking his arms through its sleeves. "So what, y'all comin' with me or not?"

Bag Man smirked as he looked at Jayvon. He admired the fact that he was willing to risk it all behind love. He did the same thing but unfortunately he still wound up losing his wife in the process. The loss of his better half brought tears to Bag Man's eyes and he dropped his head. He picked up the charm lying against his chest which was a picture of his soul-mate, Valentina. He kissed the charm and shot to his feet, taking the bamboo stick into his hands.

"I'll roll witchu, youngin'." Bag Man told him.

"G lookin' out," Jayvon dapped him up. He then looked to Augustus. "What about chu, old head? You gon' leave a young nigga hangin'?"

Augustus blew smoke from his nose and mouth as he mashed out his cigar in the clear, glass ashtray. "What the hell? I could use a lil' adventure in my life. You can deal me in, youngster." He rose, dapping up with Jayvon and patting him on his back. He then picked his piece up from the table and stuffed it inside his shoulder holster.

"That's what I'm talkin' about…Three The Hardway, baby." Jayvon grinned and shook their shoulders.

"A'ight. I know a couple of traps we can hit," Augustus said, slipping on his jacket and grabbing his apple jack.

"What chu think they're holdin'?" Bag Man asked with a wrinkled brow.

"Can't be sure, but the chump these boys work for is a mid-level player." Augustus assured him.

"Mid-level sounds good to me, anything below that ain't worth gettin' our hands dirty for." Jayvon interjected, making his way towards the door. He got the surprise of a lifetime when Dolph and Bocka walked around the corner. As if on cue, Bag Man drew his katana from his bamboo stick. Augustus upped his gun, and Jayvon upped his a second later. Dolph and Bocka stopped in their tracks.

"Whoa there, cowboys, we came in peace." Dolph assured everyone.

"And you're gonna be leavin' in about ten of 'em, pussy." Jayvon swore, looking like an angry Rottweiler by the face.

"Yew not dee only wun wit guns, ya know?" Bocka, whose dreadlocks were pulled back in a band, came off the hip with twin Desert Eagles. He pinned the first one on Jayvon and the second one on Augustus.

Right then, Chyna flew out of the hallway and into the living room.

"Y'all hold on! Put the guns down, put the goddamn guns down now." Chyna said, looking to both sides with his hands up. The opposing sides were seconds from blowing each other away and he didn't want to see that happen. He had mad love for both parties, especially his big brother.

"Chyna, if your gonna be hangin' out with these niggaz fine, but chu keep their asses the fuck away from me and mine." Jayvon said, keeping his eyes on Dolph.

"It ain't like that big bruh, we came in peace." Dolph assured him.

"What the fuck are you doin' here, homeboy? In case you didn't get the memo, I'm not feelin' you, Shabba Ranks, or y'all flockin' ass crew." Jayvon reminded him.

"I know that if I don't know anything else, but we're not here for you," Dolph told him. "We're here on the account of King Chyna. Lil' bruh told us he hadda lil' sitch, and if there's one thing we do, we take care of our own." He looked over his shoulder at Bocka. "Chill, king." Bocka hesitated before shoving his Desert Eagles inside of his shoulder holsters. "Jayvon, why don't chu tell ya manz to fall back? Me and mine don't pose a threat."

"I'm not tellin' 'em shit. Matter of fact, fuck you got in this bag?" Jayvon snatched the knapsack from Dolph and carried it over to the table.

"My fault, Dolph, man. Bro be wildin'." Chyna chimed in.

"It's a'ight, king. I knew what to expect when we rolled up in this piece." Dolph replied.

Everyone watched as Jayvon, who kept his gun pinned on Dolph, opened the knapsack and sifted through it. His forehead scrunched as he began pulling stacks of dead presidents out of it. He then dumped the contents of the knapsack onto the table top and slung it aside. A pile of money was sitting before him. Confusion registered in his eyes and he turned around to Dolph, lowering his stick at his side.

"Yo, son, what the fuck is this?" Jayvon asked curiously.

"Like I said earlier, I heard you hadda sitch and bein' that you're the young king's family, by extension that makes you our family." Dolph replied.

Jayvon looked at Chyna then at Dolph. He wasn't sure of what to say to him after his kind gesture. It wasn't long ago he and his man Bocka had nearly exchanged gunfire, so that bag getting dropped on him wasn't expected. Still, if Dolph and his man could put their differences aside, to help him get the loot up to get Chrissy back, then he was humble enough to accept their generosity.

Jayvon tucked his piece at the small of his back. He looked Dolph in his eye. "Good lookin' out. A nigga appreciate that." He tapped his fist to his chest.

"No problem, duke. The Kings look out for ours." Dolph turned to Bocka. "Ain't that right, Rasta Man?"

"No doubt." Bocka replied, mad dogging Jayvon.

Jayvon held Bocka's mad dog stare while addressing Dolph. "How much is on the table?"

"Somethin' light. A 100k to be exact." Dolph told him. "Listen, if you need more, I can—"

"Nah, this is more than enough." Jayvon spoke up. "You can expect this back with interest too."

"It's cool, bruh. Family looks out for family. Ain't that right, King Chyna?" Dolph smiled and threw his arm around Chyna's shoulders. Chyna nodded with an awkward smile then looked to his brother.

"No handouts, my G. I'ma grown ass man." Jayvon said. "I'ma see to it, you get this scratch back with interest, just like I said."

Dolph nodded and tapped his fist against his chest. "I respect that, king, real shit." There was an uncomfortable silence in the room before he spoke up again. "About that situation back at cha crib—"

"Shit is already forgotten, my nig." Jayvon cut him short.

Dolph smiled and lifted his hand. Jayvon stared at his palm as it lingered in the air, seeing it as a copperhead snake. He started to pull out his gun and blow its head off but his senses came back to him. Jayvon mustered up a weak smile and shook up with Dolph.

I don't trust you, dick sucka, but I'ma play yo' lil' game 'til you're no longer useful to me. Then I'ma blow yo' ass away, you and that Great Value Brand Bob Marley, Jayvon thought, still wearing that weak ass smile.

Dolph glanced at the time on his Rolley. "Peep, me and my manz gotta few corners to bend but if you need our assistance in gettin' your shorty back, we'd be willin' to tag along."

"Thanks but no thanks. Me and my dawgs got it from here." Jayvon assured him. Right then, Bag

Man and Augustus stepped up on both sides of him, like a couple of trained German Shepherds.

"A'ight then. Lil' bruh has my math, scream at me if you need me." Dolph smiled, adjusted his designer shades and shook up with Chyna before him and Bocka made their exit.

After Jayvon locked the door behind them, he walked upon Chyna wearing an expression that could kill.

Fuck, Chyna mouthed and shook his head. He knew Jayvon was going to get in his ass for telling the Kings his business which was stupid to him. The way he saw it, his brother needed the bread to get his girl back in one piece so he didn't see any problem with what he did.

"Son, I don't even feel like fightin' witchu over this shit." Chyna told him. "You may not be feelin' me tellin' bruh the sitch, but he came through like I knew he would. Now we can get sis back." Jayvon, wearing a solemn expression, didn't say a word as he continued in his direction. "Fuck it then, yo, you wanna rumble behind some ol' bullshit? Then I'm with all the dumb shit." He pulled his hoodie over his head and flung it aside. He pulled up his jeans and tightened his belt. Then he threw up his dukes and got into a fighting stance. "Come on then. Come on."

Once Jayvon got within firing distance, Chyna expected him to swing, but instead he did the least expected. He gave him a brotherly hug and kissed him on the side of the head.

"Thank you." Jayvon told him.

Chyna's forehead wrinkled with confusion. He slowly wrapped his arms around his brother. "You're welcome."

"I love you, lil' bruh." Jayvon told him.

"I love you too, big bruh. Son, for a minute, I thought chu was about to whip my ass." Chyna smiled.

"Nah. You came through for Chrissy. How could I be mad at that?" Jayvon smiled back. "Besides, it's 'cause of you a lotta dope boys are gonna be able to keep their trap money, maybe even their lives."

"Now, I hate to be the nigga to interrupt this beautiful family moment, but tonight I gots to be that nigga." Augustus took the cigar out of his mouth and tapped the face of his watch. It was time to make the drop and get Chrissy back.

"I hear you, unc, let's bag up this bread so we can make this move," Jayvon started loading the money back in the knapsack Dolph dropped on him.

It was time to get his queen back!

CHAPTER NINETEEN

Augustus, Chyna and Jayvon were posted up in the alley, dressed to combat the 40-below weather. Augustus took pulls from a cigar and clicked the safety on and off his gun. Bartise's people were half an hour late and he was antsy as hell. He had an uneasy feeling they may be trying to set him and the young niggaz up. If that were the case then they were in for a rude awakening, because not only was he strapped, but Chyna and his brother were also.

Augustus looked at Jayvon who was pacing the grounds with both hands in his leather jacket. Every five minutes he'd glance at the time on his cellphone and scan their surroundings. This let Augustus know he was just as antsy as he was and ready to get shit over with.

"Say, bruh, where the fuck these niggaz at, yo?" An agitated Jayvon asked.

"I don't know, youngster, but take a hit of this. It'll calm your nerves." Augustus replied, outstretching his cigar.

Jayvon waved off Augustus. "Mannn, I don't want none of yo' cheap ass cigar. That muthafucka stank somethin' awful. I'm ready for these niggaz to come with my shorty so we can roll the fuck outta here." Augustus put his cigar back in his mouth and gave him the middle finger. "Fuck you too, old nigga." He returned the gesture.

"Yo, I think I see somebody comin'," Chyna said from behind the truck where he was hidden. He was wearing a white ski mask and gripping a sawed off shotgun. Right then, the headlights of an oncoming

135

van shone on Augustus and Jayvon. Their faces balled up from the bright lights and they held their hands over their brows.

"Yeah. This is them. Y'all boys stay on point." Augustus said loud enough for only Jayvon and Chyna to hear.

"I already know where you're at with it, old head." Jayvon replied, keeping his eyes on the van. When its headlights went out, they could only see a silhouette in the driver's seat. The driver's door was thrown open and Purp jumped down to the ground. He made his way around to the front of the van, tucking his gun in his waistband. He wore a stank expression on his face as he looked Augustus and Jayvon up and down. He whistled and motioned someone over. The van's door slid open! Stutter-Box jumped out with his gun, grabbed Chrissy under her arm, and pulled her out of the van. She wore a black hood over her head and her wrists were bound behind her back. She jerked from left to right, trying to get out of Stutter-Box's grasp but he held fast.

"Chris, you a'ight?" Jayvon asked, stepping forward.

Purp threw up his hand and Jayvon froze in his tracks. "Relax, Dunn, my man didn't harm one hair on yo' bitch's head. I saw to that."

"How do we know it's her? We're not givin' you jack 'til we see her face." Augustus spoke up. He spat what was left of his cigar on the ground and mashed it out. He'd need both hands if shit went left and he had to participate in a shootout.

Purp gave Stutter-Box a nod and he snatched the black hood off Chrissy's head. Her face was scrunched and her mouth was gagged.

"See? Here—here—yo'—yo' bi—bitch is." Stutter-Box managed to say. "We—we—we didn't ha—harm a hair on—on her pretty lil'—lil'—lil'—"

Purp sighed and rolled his eyes. Stutter-Box's speech impediment irritated the fuck out of him. "Head, muthafucka, goddamn! Shit!" Purp shook his head and ran his hand down his face.

"Mannnnn, f—f—fuck—fuck you." Stutte-Box shot back.

Purp went on to address Jayvon and them. "A'ight, niggaz, where the loot at?"

"I got chu faded," Jayvon replied walking back to the truck. Chyna moved out of the way so he could pop the hatch. Jayvon tucked his pole in his waistband and grabbed the brown leather duffle bag. Slamming the hatch back, he gave Chyna a nod, letting him know to still be on point. Jayvon lugged the hefty duffle bag back around the truck where Augustus stood. The old nigga was chilling like an owl, watching everything.

Jayvon tossed the duffle bag at Purp's feet. Purp kept a close eye on his opps as he kneeled down and unzipped the duffle bag. It was loaded with bankrolls with rubber bands tangled around them. Purp sifted through the money making sure it was all legit before zipping the duffle bag back up. He grabbed the duffle bag and stood upright. He gave Stutter-Box another nod. Stutter-Box put his gun up and withdrew a bowie knife from the small of his back. He sliced off

Chrissy's gag and the duct-tape that bound her wrists.

Chrissy, who had tears in her eyes, ran towards Jayvon and jumped into his arms. Jayvon fell back against the hood of the truck, with her kissing him all over his face. A smile spread across Jayvon's lips as he received all of her affection.

"I love you. I love you. I love you." Chrissy said, still kissing him. "I love you so fuckin' much, babe. I swear. It doesn't make any sense how much I do."

"I love you too, ma." Jayvon replied, lowering her back to the ground. Cupping her face, he kissed her on the forehead and then on the lips. "Go ahead and jump in the truck. You may see lil' bruh back there at the hatch. Don't mind 'em. He's holding it down in case this sitch gets sticky." Chrissy nodded, kissed him on the cheek and hopped into the backseat of the SUV. "So we're good?" He asked Purp.

"Yeah, son, we're straight." Purp said.

"A'ight. Tell that nigga Bartise from now on to stay away from me and my family." Jayvon frowned. "As long as he does that, he and I are on good terms."

Purp side-eyed Jayvon, looking at him like he was a retarded mothafucka. "Nigga, I'm not telling Bartise shit, I'm not his secretary. Whatever you want 'em to know, you tell 'em." He pointed at Jayvon. Then motioned for Stutter-Box to follow him to the van. "Come on witcho none talkin' ass."

"Suck—suck—suck my bi—big black di—di—dick, nigga." Stutter-Box said, sheathing his bowie knife and hopping into the front passenger seat. Jayvon and Augustus stood shoulder to shoulder watching the van back up and then drive away.

"A'ight, bro bro, them niggaz gone." Jayvon called out to Chyna as he and Augustus walked back towards the SUV. Chyna came running from the rear of the vehicle, pulling his ski mask off his face.

"We're gucci, bro?" Chyna asked, scanning the alley to make sure it was kosher.

"Fa sho'." Jayvon replied, shaking up with his brother.

Jayvon drove away once everyone was inside the truck. A happy Chrissy hugged and kissed Chyna, Bag Man and Augustus for their help getting her back.

***

Jayvon started getting mad calls from fighters who wanted a shot at him after defeating Hamza. He had offers coming left and right, but he ended up going with this dude out of the Colony projects down south. Homie went by the name Savage. He was known as a knockout artist on his part of town, which made him one arrogant fuck. At least that's what he picked up in the video he sent him through Instagram. Savage was surrounded by a bunch of thug ass niggaz. They were all dressed to fight the cold weather. They were posted up in the middle of the tenements with snow pouring down. Every trap boy Savage had on deck had either a choppa or some sort of semi-automatic in their possession.

"Check dis out homeboi, I got five-hunnid thou. Yeah, ya heard right, bruh, five-hunnid thousand." Savage took a duffle bag from one of the trap boyz. He opened it and started tossing out stacks of dead presidents, calling out the amount. When he got tired of counting the dough, he said fuck it, and dumped the duffle bag out at his feet. He allowed the person filming to get a good look at all the money in the snow. "So, dere you have it, have yo' people get a hold of my people so you can get dis work." Savage flexed his muscles and then gave a demonstration of his fight skills. The trap boyz cheered him on and the video stopped.

"OG, set that shit up. I'ma beat the brakes off that fuckin' Bama." Jayvon swore before he started shadow boxing. He imagined himself giving Savage a memorable ass whipping.

"Shiiiiit, you don't gotta tell me twice. I'm already onna jack with these country boyz." Augustus said, holding his cellphone to his ear with one hand and his cigar in the other.

Augustus set up the brawl with Savage and then he made the flight arrangements. When Chyna got word of where his brother's next fight was going down, he reached out to Dolph who got in touch with his people out in North Carolina. His boy Leonidas was one of the ranking members of the King of Thieves chapter out there. He told him to see to it that his folks, Chyna and them, were well taken care of when they touched his turf. They were to be escorted from the airport to the projects and then back to the airport once their business was conducted. Leonidas promised that no harm would come to King Chyna or any of his acquaintances while they were in his city.

As soon as Jayvon and them stepped out of the Charlotte Douglas International airport, they were greeted by Leonidas and a fleet of purple and gold luxury vehicles. The man that had guaranteed their safety while in North Carolina was sitting on the hood of his '76 Buick Regal. He had one leg hanging off of his whip and was talking to whomever on his cellphone.

"Say, bruh, dis dem right here, you got their descriptions down to da T. Well, lemme properly greet da young kang and his potnas. Fa' sho'. Peace." Leonidas disconnected the call as slid off the hood of his car and pocketed his cellular. Leonidas was a five-foot-eleven brother who wore his hair shaved on the sides with box braids sprouting out of his top. His beard was so full and fluffy it made his big lips standout. Leonidas was wearing 1.5 million dollars in icy gold jewelry and a Lakers warm up tracksuit that matched perfectly with his whip. Now most would have thought the boy was out there straight stuntin, but this was an everyday thing for him and his crew. "Welcome to da land. I'm Leonidas." He shook up with everyone and exchanged pleasantries. Once he got to Chyna, he shook up with him how he did with every king he came into contact with and gave him a brotherly hug. "Good to finally meet cha, my boi, Dolph hadda lotta shit to say about cha."

"I hope it was all good." Chyna grinned.

"No doubt. Otherwise, I wouldn't be y'alls chaperone durin' your stay in my wonderful city." Leonidas assured him. He pulled back his sleeve to check the time. "I was told y'all gotta be up in Greenville for dat business inna 'bout two hours. I was thinkin' we head ova to Ma's place to grab some suppa so da champ here can get his mind right before da big fight." He referred to Jayvon. "Whadda ya say, champ? It's all on you, big dawg. Keep in mind da vittles are all on ya boi."

"Son, I'm hungry as a hostage, let's get it." Jayvon said, rubbing his growling stomach absentmindedly.

"Awright then. Let's hit it." Leonidas smacked his hands together and rubbed them in anticipation. He helped Jayvon and them load their shit inside the trunk of his Regal before hopping behind the wheel. He turned the key inside the ignition and his ride came back to life. Leonidas threw his shit in drive and pulled away from the curb. The fleet of purple and gold luxury whips pulled off behind him.

CHAPTER TWENTY

Jayvon, who was sitting in the front passenger seat, stole a glance at the side view mirror. His forehead creased when he saw the fleet of purple and gold vehicles trailing behind them. He had his ideas of what position the drivers played so he wasn't going to ask about them. Besides, he had to keep his head in the game. He had a fight coming up, and he had to be prepared if he planned to come out on top.

Leonidas saw Jayvon glancing at the fleet through his side view mirror. He knew instantly where his head was so he decided to turn the stereo's volume down and put his curiosity to bed.

"You ain't got nothin' to worry about, kang. Dem bois followin' us are for security purposes, ya unnastand me?" Leonidas said. "They gon' see to it dat we move around da city wit no hiccups. You and Kang Chyna are in good hands." Jayvon looked at him and nodded his understanding. With that out of the way, Leonidas turned the volume back up and sparked a blunt that had the whip stinking like skunk sex. After taking a few pulls he tried passing it to Jayvon, Bag Man and then Augustus. They all declined. Chyna, on the other hand, accepted the offer and got high as shit.

Leonidas adjusted the rearview mirror, to get a look at Chyna. His eyes were hooded and red-webbed.

"What chu thank, kang? That's some of North Carolina's finest." Leonidas told him.

"Oh, I most def fucks with that, wish I could take some home." Chyna admitted, rubbing his stomach.

The young nigga had the munchies and was ready to eat.

"I'ma see what I can do about sendin' you some." Leonidas said.

"I appreciate that." Chyna replied.

The Kings of Thieves parked their cars and made their way towards Ma's restaurant. Leonidas made two of the Kings post up outside the doors of the establishment to act as armed security. Once Leonidas and his guests were seated at the table, they ordered their food and beverages. Jayvon and Chyna were having a difficult time deciding what they wanted to eat so Leonidas requested his favorite dish for them. They ended up with fried catfish, cornbread, cheese grits and corn beef hash. They chopped it up about everything under the sun over their meals. Jayvon and them hadn't known Leonidas that long but they'd taken a liking to him. Their linking up with him and his crew was like cousins getting together at their grandma's house after a while.

"Hahahahaha. You New Yawk niggaz is wild, bruh. Hold on. I gotta take this." Leonidas called for everyone's silence before answering his cellphone. A serious look came over his face as he listened to what he was being told. "Damn, I mean, dang, Grandma, I forgot,"—He stole a look at his Richard Millie— "Listen, I'm entertainin' some outta town guests right now, but dat appointment is very important. I'll have some friends of mine tend to my guests while I see about pickin' you up so you can make dat appointment. Okay. I'll see you soon, young lady. I love you, too." He disconnected the call.

"Everythang good?" Jayvon asked, taking a sip of orange juice.

Leonidas nodded. "Yeah. I just forgot I was 'pose to take my ol' girl to her doctor's appointment today. She's been forgetful lately. I think she's developin' dementia."

"Man, I'm sorry to hear that." Jayvon replied.

"Yeah, me too, king." Chyna said, followed by Augustus and Bag Man.

"'Preciate dat." Leonidas placed the money for the bill on the table and rose from his chair. He gave the Kings at the table orders to make sure Jayvon and them were good at the match in his absence. He shook up with Jayvon and them before heading for the exit in a hurry. He was halfway to the door when Jayvon caught up with him.

"Look, these fools we're finna go see seem like some wild, unpredictable ass niggaz, I don't know what to expect." Jayvon told him. "I know we gotcho people watchin' our backs, but I'd feel more comfortable holding my own nuts. Nah mean?"

Leonidas frowned as he thought about the situation and massaged his chin. "Awright. I'll send one of my potnas up here wit somethin' bulletproof and a few sticks for y'all. How dat sound, bruh?"

"Lovely." Jayvon replied with a smirk. Leonidas shook up with him and jogged out Ma's, pulling out his cellular to make Jayvon's request.

Twenty minutes later

Jayvon, Chyna, Augustus, Bag Man and the kings were posted up outside of Ma's. They shot the breeze while gnawing on toothpicks or using them to pick

145

the food out of their teeth. A couple of them belched and spoke of how banging their meals were. Suddenly, the Kings went silent and reached for their waistbands. They narrowed their eyes and peered closely at an approaching vehicle.

"Aww, man, dat's King Whoadie." One of the Kings waved off the approaching triple black 2018 Lincoln Navigator. All the Kings dropped their hands from their waistband and went back to talking among each other.

The black Lincoln Navigator swung around and backed into a parking space. A five-foot-seven, brown-skinned fellow with a patchy beard hopped out of the driver's seat and made his way towards Jayvon and them. He wore gold wire-frame glasses and four gold caps on his top row of teeth. Half of his head was braided in cornrows while the other half was an afro. He was in the middle of getting his hair braided when Leonidas hit him up to drop off the bulletproof SUV.

"What's hapnin'? Which one of you niggaz Jayvon?" Whoadie asked in a New Orleans draw, looking among the lot.

"That would be me." Jayvon stepped forward, catching the keys he was thrown.

"Check dis out, baybey, I got foe wig splittas in da truck dere. FN-.357 semi-automatic handguns." Whoadie told them the models of the poles hidden in the Navigator. "All you gotta do is hit da hazard and den da AC button. Then a secret compartment gon' flip open. All foe of dem thangz gon' be in dere."

A white Mercedes-Benz truck pulled up behind Whoadie and the driver honked its horn. Whoadie threw up his hand, which translated as *give me a minute* before continuing with what he had to say.

"Anyway, I gotta get up outta here, bruh. My old lady gotta finish braidin' my shit." Whoadie chunked up the deuce before jogging over to the Benz truck and hopping into the front passenger seat. He gave the signal and the driver pulled off.

***

Augustus went down the road and made a right, traveling westbound. Seeing a five-foot-tall stone wall with Colony Apartments chiseled on it, he made a left onto the grounds of the residency that used to be known as the Washington Carver Village apartments. Jayvon rode up front with Augustus staring out of the passenger window. Once the navigation system told them they were arriving at their destination, Augustus parked the truck and killed its ignition.

Augustus, Jayvon, and Chyna focused their attention out of their windows, observing the tenement they were supposed to meet Savage. On the side of the building there were a dozen or so menacing looking men. They were smoking blunts, drinking dark liquor, and conversing. The men became eerily silent and focused their eyes on the Lincoln Navigator. The SUV's matte-black paint job and pitch-black tinted windows made it look suspicious. The men exchanged hushed words among each other before producing their assault rifles and marching towards the Lincoln Navigator.

"Don't chu think we should hit ya man up?" Chyna asked Jayvon.

147

"That's what I'm sayin', make that call, bitch."
Bag Man chimed in.

"I'm on that now." Jayvon replied, scrolling
through his contacts for Savage's number.

"Here comes the welcoming committee."
Augustus announced, putting fire to what was left of
his cigar.

"The welcoming committee? Fuck you talking
a—" Jayvon's words died in his throat when he saw
the men with assault rifles outside his window. He
pulled out his stick and chambered a bullet. Chyna
followed behind him, making sure his shit was
cocked and ready. Then there were Augustus and
Bag Man, making sure their guns were prepared for
any drama.

Chyna looked out of the back window and the
Kings were hopping out with assault rifles of their
own. Chyna had never seen so many purple bandanas
and clothing in his life. A smile spread across his lips
seeing they had an entire army backing them. He
knew then he'd never regret joining forces with the
King of Thieves.

"Say, bruh, I'm in yo' backyard," Jayvon told
Savage when he picked up his call. "Yeah. I'm inna
black Navi, pitch-black tints." He stared out of the
window at the approaching men. The leader of the
pack had on a North Carolina Tar Heels cap and a
black balaclava mask. He switched hands with his
assault rifle when his cellphone began ringing and
drew it from the recesses of his bubble jacket. He
glanced at the caller identification before hollering at
the troops.

"Y'all niggaz hold up. Dis Savage," the brother in the balaclava mask announced and answered the call. "What's up wit it, big homie? Yeah, we're out here now." He looked at the Navigator and then all the Kings posted up with the artillery. "Oooooh, awright, big dawg, we didn't know who deez niggaz was dat pulled up. We were 'bouta roast deez trucks they got out here. I feel ya. Peace." He disconnected the call. Then he addressed his flock. "Yo, dat was big homie, deez niggaz rollin' wit homeboi dats 'pose to throw down wit Savage fa dat bag so y'all bois fall back." He stashed his cellular back inside of his bubble jacket. Then he addressed Jayvon and them. "It's all good fam, da big homie says y'all here fa dat brawl. Y'all can hop out and come holla. Big dawg on his way down now."

Jayvon and them jumped out of the Lincoln Navigator. Bag Man popped the hatch and grabbed a big leather duffle bag. After slamming the hatch shut, he linked back up with the crew and they walked over to homie in the North Carolina cap and balaclava mask. He apologized for the misunderstanding, introduced himself as LayLow and shook up with all of them.

"It's all goodie, my nigga, where that nigga Savage at though? I've gotta ass whippin' for 'em that's been sitting on layaway for a while now." Jayvon said, half-jokingly. Everyone on his side laughed or smirked while LayLow and his troops scowled behind their masks. "You country boyz don't have a sense of humor, do you?"

"Nah. We take everythang serious 'round here, my nigga, and once I'm done poundin' ya face into burger, you will too. Believe dat, lil' nigga." A commanding voice came from over LayLow's shoulder. When everyone looked in the direction it came from there stood a five-foot-eleven brother who was built like a wrestler. He had coco-brown skin and a long fluffy beard. He donned a fox fur, Russian Ushanka hat and a copper-brown shearling winter jacket with a fur collar. He was flanked by two sexy ass hood bitchez who were dressed identical to him. The only difference being their hats and jackets were black. Only one of them was holding a designer duffle bag.

Jayvon grinned and adjusted his beanie over his ears. "I hear you, Mr. Savage, but chu gon' have to make me a believer." Savage nodded in agreement. "Now, is that my winnings in that bag yo' shorty's holding?"

"Your winnings? You cocky lil' shit. Y'all hear dis mothafucka?" Savage asked the women standing on the sides of him.

"Unh, huh. He's talm 'bouta whole bunch of nothin', daddy." One of the sexy bitchez replied.

"Yep. I say you shut his big city ass up by beatin' nem down." The other sexy bitch added.

"Whadda ya say, city boy? Shall we get on wit dee activities?" Savage asked Jayvon.

Right then, the wind kicked up and snowflakes swirled around them.

CHAPTER TWENTY ONE

Bap!Wop!Bwrack!

Blood landed on the snow creating a cherry slushy. Savage's body landed on top of it. He was battered, bruised, bleeding and ugly. He was exhausted but he had to get up. His reputation was on the line. He wouldn't be able to walk around the hood with his head up if he didn't come out on top.

Jayvon, who had a knot on his forehead and a blood clot in his right eye, bounced around with his busted, bloody knuckles up. He spat a bloody loogie on the ground and waited for Savage to get up.

Jayvon could feel the heat from Savage's trap boys on him. He knew if it wasn't for the Kings being there to hold him down they would have bodied him and ran off with his bag by now. Savage was a hardcore, penitentiary nigga that had been through mad shit, in and out of the streets. He and his brethren underestimated Jayvon and now they were paying the price for it.

"Come on, Savage, whip his ass!" One of the trap boys shouted.

"Show his bitch-ass how project babies get down!" A second trap boy shouted.

"Smash dis fuck boi, big homie!" A third trap boy shouted.

The trap boys and residents of the projects were in an uproar. They wanted Jayvon's blood on the snow. He'd made the man they viewed as god look like a mortal and that hurt.

"I think it's safe to say you took that ass whippin' off layaway." Jayvon smiled down at Savage.

"Y'all stand ready, the natives are gettin' hostile." Augustus told Bag Man and Chyna in a hushed tone.

"I see." Bag Man said, looking around at all the angry faces.

"If it goes down then what's the move?" Chyna asked, keeping his eyes on the opps.

"First off, we lay down any of these project niggaz that try to take a shot at your brother. Then we go after that bag of loot that young tender has over there." Augustus nodded to Savage's sexy ass hood bitch with the designer bag. "While Leonidas's people are exchanging fire with these fools, we make a fast break for the truck and hightail it up outta here."

"Sounds like a plan." Chyna said.

"Maybe we should spread the word to the Kings." Bag Man suggested. He looked at Augustus. Augustus nodded and whispered his plan to the King he believed was second in command. He in turn, whispered to another King and the word spread among his gang like wildfire.

The trap boys and the residents of the projects cheered joyfully when Savage got back up. Unbeknownst to everyone, he took a red capsule the size of a horse pill from the small pocket of his jeans and slipped it in his mouth. He then threw up his dukes and stalked towards Jayvon.

"'Bout time you gotcho big ass up." Jayvon smirked.

"Keep talkin', city boy, dis shit ain't over by a long shot." Savage's face twisted in anger and he clenched his jaws.

I'm God in dees projects, and I'll be damned if I let dis lil' mothafucka make me look like anythang less.

Jayvon gave Savage a cold ass three piece that made his legs buckle. He followed up with an overhand right and then a left. Savage ducked them both, came back up and blew a red powder into his face.

"Aaaah!" Jayvon squenched his eyes as he screamed. The powder burned like the hottest mace. His pupils felt like they were on fire. His eyes were watery and all he could see was a red haze.

"Something's up?" Bag Man told Chyna, keeping his eyes on the brawl.

"I think that dirty muthafucka threw something in bro's eyes." Chyna replied, keeping his eyes on the brawl as well.

"Are you sure? I didn't see 'em throw anything" Augustus said.

"Can't be sure, but what other reason could be the cause of bruh losin' his sight all of a sudden?" Chyna asked. He went to draw his piece from his waistband but Augustus grabbed his wrist before he could clear it.

"Not just yet, young blood, let's see how this plays out." Augustus told him. "We don't know exactly what happened so if you set it off now, it won't look right. You understand?" Chyna took a deep breath and nodded. He knew Augustus was kicking some real shit to him so he decided to fall back and follow the old nigga's lead.

What the fuck, son? I can't see! I can't see jack shit, Jayvon thought, blinking his eyes rapidly and swinging blindly. Every time one of his punches failed to connect, Savage fired on him as hard as he could, bruising his face black and blue.

"Da tables have turned on yo' ho-ass, city boy." Savage spat blood on the snow and laughed heartily. He casually walked up on Jayvon throwing punch after punch, making him stagger backwards.

"Savage, Savage, Savage, Savage!" The trap boys and residents chanted.

Savage smiled joyously and threw his hands up and down. This was his way of telling them to raise their voices higher and higher. Meanwhile, Jayvon had his hands held in front of him and was slowly walking back. The red powder had completely blinded him, leaving him at Savage's mercy.

Having gotten enough praise from his audience, Savage set his sight back on Jayvon and smiled fiendishly. He charged at him like a field goal kicker and launched his knee into his stomach. Jayvon's eyes bubbled as he was lifted off his boots. He dropped to his hands and knees. His abs were sore as a bitch and he was grimacing. He coughed up mucus and spat on the ground.

Savage walked around Jayvon as he got upon one knee in an attempt to get back up. He waited until he was about to stand upright and then he kicked him in the side of the head. Jayvon did a 360° turn in mid-air and landed on his stomach.

"Finish him! Finish him! Finish him!" The trap boys and residents chanted.

Grabbing Jayvon by the back of his wife beater, Savage pulled him up to his hands and knees, dog walking him towards one of the buildings, to smash his face into it. Suddenly, Jayvon halted and refused to budge. Savage tried pulling him along but he held fast. Savage tried to put him in a chokehold and that's when things took a turn for the worse. Abruptly, Jayvon sunk his teeth into Savage's forearm and shook his head like a mean ass Rottweiler.

"Gaaaaaaah!" Savage screamed like he was being stabbed to death. He tried gouging out Jayvon's eyes, but that just made him angrier. Jayvon bit down harder, shaking his head faster and growling. Blood poured out of Savage's wound as he screamed loud enough for the angels in heaven to hear him. Nearly everyone looking at the level of savagery Jayvon displayed cringed and looked away. Jayvon had turned into a wild animal before their very eyes. "Get dis mothafucka off me, get 'em off!"

The trap boys went to do as ordered, but everyone that was there for Jayvon drew down on them. With them having the drop on the trap boys, all they could do was fall back and let the fight play out.

"Grrrrr!" Jayvon's head flew back as he came away with a chunk of meat from Savage's arm. He spat it on the snow and mad dogged Savage. He looked like a zombie with blood dripping from his chin. Although Jayvon had been blinded by the powder he could still hear. Down on his hands and knees, he listened closely to Savage's screaming to locate him. Once he pinpointed where he stood, Jayvon took off running and tackled him. He lifted him three feet off the ground and slammed him on his back.

Savage lay on his back in pain, feeling like his spine was broken. Jayvon straddled him and felt up his body until he located his face. He balled his fists and rained down blows on his face, rearranging it. With every punch that connected, blood clung to Jayvon's face and chest.

"Ah shit, bitch 'bouta kill this nigga." Bag Man said, running towards Jayvon. Still holding his gun, he grabbed Jayvon under his arms and pulled him off of Savage. Jayvon twisted and turned in his arms. He kicked and screamed like a toddler throwing a tantrum.

"Lemme go, lemme go!" Jayvon hollered, desperate to finish what he started.

Savage lay in the snow barely conscious moaning. His face was busted, swollen and bloody. He was so fucked up his own mother wouldn't recognize him.

LayLow looked at the sexy hood bitchez that had Savage's designer bag full of dead faces. He gave them a head nod. They slowly stepped back from all the commotion and took off running in the opposite direction. They bent the corner of one of the buildings and ran dead smack into Leonidas. He was flanked by an army of heavily armed Kings and they looked like they meant business.

"And just where do you, two low rent, fake bougie bitchez thank you're goin'? Gemme dat gotdamn bag." Leonidas snatched the designer bag and peered inside. "Awright, you hoes beat it foe I change my mind." He threw his head over his shoulder and they took off.

Leonidas switched hands with the designer bag. Using his gun, he motioned for the Kings to follow him as he ran towards the drama. When Leonidas and the Kings reached the battle ground, LayLow and the troops were lying on their stomachs with their fingers interlocked behind their heads. The other Kings were walking among them picking up their weapons. Bag Man and Chyna were tending to Jayvon who appeared to have something in his eyes.

Leonidas whistled for their attention as he held up the designer bag. He and Chyna met halfway. He gave him the designer bag and he shook up with him. Then Chyna gave him a rundown of what happened in his absence. Leonidas scowled and looked around at all the fools lying at his sneakers.

"I knew somethin' foul was gon' happen down here, which is why once big mama's doctor's appointment was ova, I rallied some mo' of my guys and made my way ova here." Leonidas told him. "Look, I gotta private jet y'all can hop on. I'ma holla at my pilot and tell 'em to get it prepared. Gather yo' fam so y'all can get up out dis bitch."

Chyna nodded and shook up with him again before running off to get the others. Leonidas pulled out his cellular and hit his pilot. He watched as Chyna and them helped Jayvon over in his direction. He looked over the grounds, to find the residents with their hands up and some of his Kings running the pockets of Savage's trap boys.

"Aye, man, y'all already took our guns and now y'all robbin' us?" One of the trap boys complained.

"Shut the fuck up!" One of the Kings kicked him in the side, making him grumble in pain. Smiling, he removed a fat ass knot of wrinkled bills from his pocket and slipped it into his own. "We're not called da King of Thieves fa nothin'."

157

"Awright, I'ma send my people dere now. One thousand." Leonidas disconnected the call and told Chyna and them the address where the private jet would be waiting for them.

"Fuck, son, this shit burning my eyes, I need some water." Jayvon said with a scrunched nose and tear streaked cheeks.

"Nah, you need some milk, my nigga. Trust me. It'll do da trick." Leonidas assured him.

"I saw a Circle K on our way up here. We can stop by there on our way to your private jet." Augustus chimed in.

"Y'all stashed dem sticks back in dat secret compartment Kang Whoadie hipped y'all to. I'll have one of my people pick up da truck later." Leonidas told them.

"Good lookin' out, king." Chyna shook up with Leonidas and gave him a half hug.

"Don't mention it, kang. I'm sho' by now you know how we look out foe each other in dis royal family." Leonidas replied before going on to shake up with the rest of the gang.

***

Augustus drove to Circle K where he bought milk and everything else needed to clean Jayvon's wounds and patch him up. As soon as they reached the hangar where Leonidas's private jet was waiting for them, they deposited the guns inside of the truck's secret compartment and jumped out. Once they were all aboard the aircraft, the pilot cranked up its engine and the blades spun until they were moving so fast they were blurs. The jet drove out of the hangar, gathering speed before slowly ascending into the sky.

CHAPTER TWENTY TWO

Chrissy was on the couch in her robe sipping wine and watching *All the Queens Men* when she heard someone knocking at the door. She sat her glass down and tied her up her robe. She stole a glance through the peephole and unlocked the door. Chyna and Jayvon walked through the door and she locked it behind them. Chyna dumped the designer bag of winnings on the kitchen table and recovered a money counter.

Chrissy frowned seeing the bumps and bruises Jayvon had accumulated in his absence. Cupping his face, she took stock of his damage with a concerned look on her face.

"Oh my God, bae, are you okay?" Chrissy asked.

"Yeah, I'm gucci, Doll," Jayvon replied, kissing her lips.

Chyna placed the money counter on the kitchen table and unzipped the designer bag. "You should see the other nigga, sis," He smiled, grabbing a stack of dead presidents from the bag.

"Where'd you get this hat from?" Chrissy said, taking Savage's hat from Jayvon's head and placing it on her own. She spun around and modeled it in the full length mirror, in the corner of the living room.

"It belonged to the nigga I fought. It's mine now though." Jayvon replied, looking at her model Savage's hat.

Chrissy saw Chyna counting up the bread from the designer bag. Her brows wrinkled as she turned around. "Y'all gotta be crazy to bring alla that loot up in this grimey ass neighborhood. Every dope fiend and stickup kid within a two block radius will be lookin' to kill you over that money."

"Baby girl, I'm not sweating a damn thang. They better remember one thang if they come after mine," Jayvon said, allowing Chrissy to take Savage's jacket off his shoulders. He turned around to her strapped, a nickel-plated Desert Eagle in each hand. She hadn't noticed the sticks because the jacket had hidden them. "They gotta bring ass to get some."

"You muthafuckin' right. And while they're tryna get at big bro for this chicken, lil' bruh gon' come outta nowhere giving niggaz the blues." Chyna held up his gun briefly and then activated the money counter. The sound of cash shuffling through the machine filled the living room.

Jayvon sat his Desert Eagles on the kitchen table and pulled out a chair. He pulled Chrissy over onto his lap and tongued her down. He ran his hand up and down her thigh while she fixed Savage's hat on her head. "That's a big bag we've got there, Doll. Even after I kicked Bag Man his training fee and the old man his management fee. Then what I blessed lil' bruh with. We still sittin' on, like, four-hundred and twenty or so."

"Dollars?" Chrissy asked, lying against him and rubbing his chest.

Jayvon frowned. "Fuck no. My black ass didn't travel alla way to the dirty for a few hundoes. I'm talkin' thousands of dollars."

"Balllllllllllin'!" Chyna echoed Jim Jones and shot an imaginary jumper.

"My baby checkin' a bag then. That's what I'm talkin' about, boo." She kissed him under his chin and the side of his neck.

"Now that we're getting to this money, we can't keep slummin'." Jayvon told her, rubbing and gently pinching her thigh.

"What chu mean?" Chrissy's forehead crinkled.

"I'm saying we get outta the hood and go somewhere safer. Nah mean?" Jayvon said.

Chrissy popped up with excitement in her eyes. "Oooh, oooh, oooh, does this mean I get to go furniture shoppin'?"

"Yep. But don't go too crazy 'cause wherever we move we'll be moving again soon after." Jayvon told her. "I plan on coppin' a mansion, and I believe I can do it as long as I keep getting purses like this last one I got."

Chrissy shouted joyfully and clapped her hands. "Ooooh, baby, I cannot wait to see what our new place is gonna look like."

"Me either." Jayvon replied, with her kissing and hugging him.

After whipping Savages's ass, Jayvon went on a crazy winning spree, knocking mad niggaz' dicks in the dirt. No matter the size or skill set, somehow Jayvon managed to always come out on top. With his newfound stardom came money and lots of it. In fact, seemingly overnight he became a millionaire and a celebrity in the underground fighting circuit.

Bartise went through fighters like prostitutes went through trick ass niggaz. Every fighter he sent at Jayvon met their downfall. Time and time again the poor kid from Bed-Stuy Do or Die proved himself worthy. Bartise got so desperate that he sent Purp and Stutter-Box to proposition him again. He put up $1,500,000 dollars to have Jayvon come fight for him but he turned him down. Each and every time Purp and Stutter-Box approached Jayvon offering larger and larger sums of cash that Bartise thought he'd take, but he always turned it down. Needless to say, Bartise was as bitter as a baby mama whose baby's daddy had moved on with another woman. His riches had made him arrogant and egotistical. He felt like his money could afford him anything, but Jayvon proved otherwise.

***

Draco slung a sack of commissary goods over his shoulder as he walked out the cell of one of the convicts his crew was extorting. He made his way down the tier reciting the lyrics to a Lil' Durk. Feeling a pair of eyes on him, he turned around and the guy he'd relieved of a few items snatched his head back in his cell. Smirking, Draco turned back around, shaking his head and going about his business.

"Bitch ass nigga. If homie had the balls to fight back I may have let 'em keep some of this shit." Draco said, like he was talking to someone beside him. He thought about the commissary he'd come up on and how he was going to divide it among his crew. Although it was deemed as disrespectful, Draco glanced in the cells he passed on his way down the tier, looking for anything worth strong arming from other inmates. He stole a look inside one particular cell of a man he knew for a fact was with the shits.

Though the man had a fierce reputation, if he had anything of value, Draco was willing to bump heads with him and whomever else.

Trick stood at the commode relieving his bladder. He was so focused he didn't notice Draco taking inventory of the goods in his cell. Draco saw a television-set, mad hygiene products, and other items he deemed valuable.

Yeah, I'm definitely gon' have to see what this moreno's hittin' foe, Draco thought, smiling devilishly and massaging his chin.

Draco's forehead wrinkled when he spotted a picture on the wall of Trick's cell. It was of Trick, a woman he assumed was his lady, and two young men. Draco recognized both of the young men. In fact, he knew one of them personally because he'd ran off with a package of drugs he'd given him to sell.

Chyna! Lil' bitch-ass nigga owes me bread, Draco thought with a scowl, clenching his sack tighter. *Bloody Knuckles. That's the moreno that crushed Hamza in that match a while back.*

"Say, bruh, mind yo' fuckin' eyes 'fore I pluck 'em outta ya head!" Trick approached the bars of his cell, hiding something behind his back. Draco was so tangled in his thoughts he hadn't noticed Trick had flushed the toilet and retrieved his banger.

"My bad, pa, nice lookin' familia." Draco nodded to the picture of Trick's family.

"Whatever, shawty, keep dat shit pushin'." Trick replied with a mad dog stare, itching to sink his shank in Draco's kidneys.

Draco smirked and nodded as he came down the tiers' steps. Normally when a nigga got at him like Trick had, he'd go get his banger and make a movie with him, but their brief interaction got him thinking.

Where the fuck this nigga goin'? Draco thought when DeMozzio crossed his path. He called after him and he turned around. "Where you headed, my boy?" Draco shook up with him.

"'Bouta hit up my abuela. It's her birthday." DeMozzio replied. "Why? What's up?"

"You remember when I promised you we'd live like kings behind these walls?" Draco threw his arm around DeMozzio's shoulders as he walked beside him.

"Yeah, hermano, I remember." DeMozzio nodded, recalling the night the promise was made.

"Well, I've gotta plan, that's gonna guarantee that promise is kept."

CHAPTER TWENTY THREE

Ever since Chyna had gotten down with the Kings of Thieves life had been good. Not only did he have his own crib, but he kept him and Jayvon's old brownstone. He had more jewelry than this era's rappers, his pockets were fatter than Loni Love, and he had a whip for nearly every day of the week. Chyna was getting to it but his money paled in comparison to what Jayvon had. Still, knowing how far they'd come, he had to salute his brother's level of success.

Since Dolph had taken it upon himself to sponsor Chyna into the King of Thieves, Chyna decided to do the same with a young nigga he'd taken a liking to. The little homie reminded Chyna a lot of himself. Hell, their lives nearly mirrored each other down to the T. Chyna studied the kid and gave him pointers here and there on how to move and handle certain situations. He laid out an array of tests he passed with flying colors. Now, the time came for the upstart to prove himself like Chyna had to with Dolph. If he handled this next test accordingly, then he was going to be welcoming him into the family.

Chyna took a few pulls from an overstuff blunt of OG Kush before passing it to D'Anthony. He hopped off the hood of his 1969 Chevy Camaro on gleaming gold rims and took the purple bandana from his right back pocket. He smiled at the classic beauty when he saw his reflection on its chameleon paint. The color of his new toy teetered between blue and purple under the street lights. The paint job ran him just shy of ten racks but it was well worth it.

"Yo, son, this one bad ass bitch, I can't wait to ride like this. I betchu get mad pussy wit this joint." D'Anthony told Chyna as he walked around the Chevy Camaro, taking in the appearance of the tricked-out ride.

"I do a'ight, B." Chyna smiled as he leaned against the side of his whip. He was capping about doing alright with the shorties though. Everything from hood rats to independent business women was on his dick. He had to fight those hoes off with a stick.

"A'ight, my ass. I see you doin' yo' thang, nigga. Salute." D'Anthony shook up with Chyna and passed the blunt back.

Chyna took a few pulls and blew a cloud of smoke up into the air. "I'm doing my thang. I ain't even gon' front on you, kid, I'm shining. And inna minute, if you come through how you 'pose to, you gon' be shining too."

"I know, big bruh, I can't wait to get money with y'all niggaz." D'Anthony smiled, rubbing his hands together like he was trying to keep warm. He was more so thinking about the dough he stood to make once the Kings of Thieves put him on.

Chyna took in D'Anthony from head to toe. His drip wasn't it. Little homie had on a navy blue Yankees baseball cap, a dingy oversized hoodie and some worn out Timbs that were entirely too big. In fact, those shits were so big he had to stuff them with socks just so he could fit them.

Chyna nodded with a smirk. "Yo' time is coming, son, trust the process."

A cellphone rung. Chyna went to reach for his cell, but D'Anthony drew his first, informing him that it was actually someone calling him. Chyna went on smoking his blunt and taking in his surroundings. He tried his best to give his little homie privacy, but from his range he couldn't help eavesdropping.

"Ma, you worry too much. I'm good. I'm just out here kickin' it wit my big bruh." D'Anthony told his mother. Chyna looked up at him with a grin. He loved the fact he had someone looking up to him like he looked up to Jayvon growing up. It was like it gave his life meaning and purpose.

D'Anthony walked what he thought was out of earshot of Chyna for some privacy. He didn't have a clue that Chyna could still hear him from where he was standing. D'Anthony started talking to his little brothers and sister about food. They complained of how hungry they were and asked if he could bring them something to eat.

"I'ma see what I can do about gathering up y'all some grub. It won't be Mickey D's or nothing like that, but it will be something. A'ight. Tell ma I'll be up there inna minute. Love y'all. One." D'Anthony disconnected the call and walked back up to Chyna. "My bad, bro, that was Maduke's and the fam."

Chyna nodded his understanding. "Yo, how come you haven't properly introduced me to yo' people, kid? I feel like I know 'em as much as I've talked to 'em on the jack, but I've never laid eyes on 'em. What? You're ashamed of me or something, yo'?"

"Nah, nah, big homie, it's nothin' like that. It's just that, it's just that..." D'Anthony dropped his head and stuck his hands inside of his pockets. Chyna saw the embarrassment and shame written across his face. He knew more than likely that the little nigga was ashamed of how his place looked, and there being a lack of food in the frig. He came up in the struggle so he knew how the youngin' felt.

"It's all good, lil' one, I've been there before. I know how it is. Trust me." Chyna told him before flicking what was left of the blunt aside. He pulled a wad of bluish green dead faces from his pocket and counted off three one hundred dollar bills.

D'Anthony shook his head and pushed Chyna's money away. "Nah, I'm not taking no bread from you, bro. This iPhone was enough."

"Lil' bruh, fuck what chu talking about. You gon' take this and make sho' ya moms and them babies up there eat." Chyna yanked him forward and stuffed the three hundred dollars inside of his pocket. He then checked the time on his icy AP and walked around to the driver side of his Chevy. He pulled out his piece from his waistband so it wouldn't dig into his hip. He snatched open the door and was about to hop in when D'Anthony called after him. Chyna looked up as the young nigga jogged over to him and extended his hand. They shook up and embraced like brothers who hadn't seen each other in a while.

"Thank you. I'll never, ever forget what you've done for me and mine. I love you, big bruh, no cap." D'Anthony said with teary eyes, holding Chyna in his embrace.

"I love you too, B. We are family so I'ma always hold you down." Chyna replied. He had mad love for shorty. He was his little man, like he was Dolph's

169

little man. If it came down to it he'd bust his gun, lay his life down and/or do a bid for him.

"Vise versa. Loyalty." D'Anthony lifted his hoodie to show "Loyalty" inked across his stomach in Old English letters.

"Loyalty." Chyna replied, lifting up his shirt to reveal the same tattoo across his stomach. They'd gotten the ink on his birthday. A day that they both shared.

Chyna cranked up his whip, revved it up and then drove away. D'Anthony stood in the street watching the Chevy Camaro grow small until it disappeared.

***

Chrissy came through the door after a long day of shopping on Fifth Avenue. She crooned lowly as she danced over the threshold with her arms filled with bags. She bumped the door closed with her hips, locked all the locks and turned around.

"Aaaaaah!" Chrissy screamed and dropped her bags. She went to draw the gun from her purse but the man perched on her staircase was quicker on the draw. He held her at gunpoint as he rose to his feet with a box tucked under his arm.

"Be easy, chica, I didn't come here to harm you. My people just wanted me to make sure you get this package." The man spoke from behind a clown mask. "Once it's in your hands, I'll be on my way."

"What is it?"

The masked man shrugged. "I'ma soldier. I carry out orders. I don't ask questions."

The masked man held the box out to her and she hesitantly took it. He walked out of the mansion, pulling the door closed behind him. Chrissy shook the box and listened for ticking. There wasn't any. She was curious as to what was inside the box so she used one of the keys on her ring to slice it open.

***

Shorty removed his clown mask and sat it on the passenger seat. He glanced up at the rearview mirror and watched the mansion grow smaller the further he drove. He placed his cellular on the dashboard attachment, scrolled through his contacts, and pressed the number he was looking for.

"Yeah?" Draco picked up on the second ring.

"They have it." Shorty said before disconnecting the call.

Meanwhile

"Aaaaaaaaah!" Jayvon hollered so loud his uvula shook crazily. Thor's face was a mask of hatred as he squeezed Jayvon's body into his own. The sound of his opponent's bones cracking made him smile.

"You hear that, Tar Baby? Your bones are gonna snap any minute now. Grrrrr." Thor squeezed him tighter, making his face ball up painfully. Jayvon's head was hanging over his back so he could see the crowd upside down. He saw people in the audience egging Thor to crush him while others cheered him on to fight. Out of everyone, Bag Man stood out the most. He instructed him on what he should do. Jayvon frowned trying to figure out what he had in mind. Suddenly it dawned on him and he went into action.

Jayvon threw his head up and brought both of his hands around fast. His hands collided with Thor's ears and he roared like a grizzly with its paw in a bear trap. Thor dropped Jayvon and staggered backwards, holding his aching ears. Jayvon was on his bending knees holding his sides, wincing. He looked at the pained expression on Thor's face and then over his shoulder at Bag Man. Bag Man cupped his hands around his mouth and shouted something at him. He couldn't hear him over the noisy audience at first, but then he came in loud and clear.

"What're you waiting for, bitch? Put his big ass down!"

Jayvon went charging at Thor. When he'd gotten close enough Thor swung at him. Jayvon slid between his legs like a baseball player, sliding to home base. He punched him in his balls so hard the audience cringed and said, "oooooooh". Thor's face turned red and his eyes widened. He doubled over, grabbing his precious jewels. Jayvon grabbed him by his waist from behind. Grunting, he lifted him up and dumped him on his head. Jayvon lay next to Thor breathing heavily, staring up at the sky. Not only was he tired, he was aching all over. He listened to the Skinheads yell for Thor to get up but he was knocked out cold. The referee counted him out and then announced Jayvon as the winner.

CHAPTER TWENTY FOUR

Everyone that placed a bet on Jayvon to win rushed the floor. They picked Jayvon up and held him high over their heads. He winced and smiled, loving the praise he was receiving. He looked over his shoulder and saw Bag Man shaking up a bottle of Ace of Spade. He smiled happily as he sprayed Jayvon and his fans.

"I knew you could do it, bitch. I'm finna go get our coins." Bag Man passed him the golden bottle and ran off to collect their winnings.

The crowd set Jayvon down and he took the champagne to the head thirstily. He wiped the wetness from his chin and took the time to sign autographs. He signed his signature on a couple of white chicks' tits. Then he took a few flicks with some fans of his. He exchanged daps and hugs with a few others before they went to watch the next fight. By the time the crowd cleared, Bag Man was waltzing back over with two big ass duffle bags. He had his piece tucked in the front of his jeans, so any jack boys watching would think twice about trying him. He took a cautious look around before he handed one of the duffle bags to Jayvon. Side by side, they made their way towards the parking lot.

"Yo, son, we're gonna hire some bodyguards to roll with us after this. After I've finished whippin' on these fools, I'm not in the mood to squabble with some knuckleheads who tryna take what I've earned. Ya heard?" Jayvon told him, wincing. He took the pole Bag Man passed him and held it at his side. He kept a close eye on his surroundings as they walked to their ride.

"Yeah, bitch, I hear you." Bag Man replied. "What chu thank about us keeping it in the family, and bringing in some of those King of Thieves niggaz baby bro rolls with? I'm sure they don't mind busting their guns for us."

"Man, hell fuckin' naw, I don't trust nan one of them sticky fingered bandits." Jayvon said. "Thieving muthafuckaz may try to take my shit. God forbid that happens, 'cause on everythang I love, I'd crush their entire crew behind mine."

Augustus smoked one of his cheap ass cigars while sitting behind the wheel of the bulletproof Lincoln Navigator. Jayvon and Bag Man dumped their duffle bags into the hatch and hopped into the backseat. Augustus started up the truck, backed out and drove away.

Jayvon pulled out his cellphone and hit up Chyna. "What up, baby boy?"

"Damn, son, you're sounding real down and out. You tooka L?" Chyna asked.

"Yeah, man. Can't win 'em all."

"It's all good, big bruh. You'll get 'em next time."

"Syke, I won you bitch-ass nigga! Aaaaaahhh!" Jayvon hollered, punching the ceiling repeatedly.

"Aaaaaaaaahhhh!" Chyna hollered back into the cellphone. Jayvon held his cellular to Bag Man's mouth and he hollered like they had into the receiver. "Yo, bro, we've gotta celebrate tonight. I know you got unc there witchu so call up sis. Everythang on me, my nigga."

"Fa' sho', lil' bruh. We're on tonight."

"I love you, bro."

"I love you more, my G. I'ma holla at chu once everyone is ready."

"A'ight. One hunnit."

As soon as Chyna hung up, Jayvon's cellphone was ringing again. He smiled when he saw "Wifey" on the display. He knew it was his baby—Chrissy.

"Who dat?" Bag Man inquired.

"The wife. So shhhhh," Jayvon held his finger to his lips. "What's up, boo? How—"

"Baby, come home quick!" Chrissy said in a panic.

Jayvon's heart skipped a beat when heard the worry in her voice. A thousand scenarios went through his mind and neither of them were good.

"What's the matter, Doll Face?" Jayvon asked.

"It's your—it's your father, baby." Chrissy cried.

"What about my pops? Chris, what the fuck is goin' on?" Jayvon asked with concern. His heart was beating fast and he was afraid of what she might say next.

"Just hurry home." Chrissy replied before disconnecting the call.

"Hello? Hello? Chris? Chris! Shiiit!" Jayvon cussed with frustration.

"What's the matter, bitch?" Bag Man asked, with a wrinkled brow.

"I can't say for sure, but something's up with my old man. Yo, floor this muthafucka, G, we've gotta make it to the crib, asap." Jayvon told Augustus. He made sure his stick was fully loaded before cocking it back. He called Chyna back and told him to meet him at his place. While they were chopping it up, Bag Man clicked the safety off his piece and slipped it back inside of his jacket.

Augustus activated his stash spot. A black semi-automatic pistol came down out of a secret compartment like a soda can from a vending machine. He placed the piece in his lap, strapped the seatbelt across his chest and mashed out. He drove like an ambulance driver with a dying man aboard, dipping in and out of lanes. He ran a couple red lights and nearly ran a pedestrian over.

***

The Lincoln Navigator halted in front of Jayvon's mansion. Chyna's Chevy pulled up right behind it. The doors of the vehicles popped open and everyone hopped out. They closed their doors and grouped up. Jayvon, holding his gun, whispered to Bag Man, Chyna and Augustus where he wanted them to enter the mansion. They gave a knowing nod and spread out. Jayvon pressed his ear against the front door and listened to what was going on inside.When he didn't hear anything, he gently turned the doorknob and crept inside. All the lights were out and the place was still. Jayvon closed the front door quietly and made his way through the mansion. He came across Augustus, Chyna and Bag Man who were moving about stealthily. They nearly popped each other thinking the other was the opposition. Sighing, came together and crept toward the living room.

Jayvon was the first man to enter the living room, swaying his gun around. When he didn't see anyone that posed a threat, he lowered his piece and addressed Chrissy. "Baby, what's the matter?"

Chrissy ran over to Jayvon and hugged him. "Bae, it's your father. Look." She showed him the iPhone that Shorty personally delivered to their mansion.

Augustus, Bag Man and Chyna greeted Chrissy with a quick hug. Jayvon tucked his gun and looked at the iPhone. Chrissy and the boys peered over his shoulders at the device's screen. They were shocked by the imagery.

Trick hung completely naked from the neck of the showerhead by his wrists. His face was bruised, swollen and bloody. His hairy chest expanded and shrunk with every raspy breath. He'd put up one hell of a fight, but the fools that came for him proved to be more than he could handle.

Standing on either side of Trick were Draco, DeMozzio and six other hittaz. Their faces and hands were wrapped in dingy bed sheets that made them look like mummies. Their uniforms were spotted with blood and so were the water pipes in their hands.

"Bloody Knuckles, I gotta say I'ma huge fan. A huge, huge fan, bro." Draco smiled. "I've been following your career. You shot to the top rather quickly. Congratulations, papi." He clapped his hands but Jayvon wasn't moved.

"My nigga, what the fuck is all this about?" Jayvon frowned, wishing he could whoop his ass.

"This is all about money, my boy." Draco replied.

"Fuck 'em! Fuck these spics, Scrap!" Trick shouted, blood and spit flying from his lips. "Don't give 'em nothin'! Not one fuckin' penny, son! I'd rather die than—"

Draco struck Trick with his pipe, splitting his head to the white meat and knocking him out cold. Blood ran down the side of his face and splashed on the floor.

"You muthafucka, I'm gonna rip your fuckin' heart out! You hear me, nigga?" Chyna shouted at Draco. He was teary-eyed and enraged. Bag Man had to grab him before he could snatch the cellphone from Jayvon.

Jayvon's face twisted and he balled his fist. Tears slid down his cheeks. Chrissy hugged him to provide some sort of comfort. "I swear on everythang I love, if you touch 'em again, I'm gonna—" Draco lifted his pipe, threatening to strike Trick in the head again. "No! Stop. Stop. Don't!"

"You come at me like that again, and me and my carnales are gonna beat this old ass nigga to death. You got that?" Draco threatened.

Taking the time to calm down, Jayvon nodded his understanding. "Look, bruh, you said this is about money, right? Just tell me how much you want, and I'ma make sure you get it. Just don't hurt my pops— please."

There was a momentary pause before Draco answered Jayvon, "Cinco millones de dólares."

"I don't speak Spanish! What the fuck does that mean?" Jayvon said, looking at everyone on his end of the cellphone.

"Baby, that's five million dollars." Chrissy told him.

Five million dollars? I don't have that kinda bread, Jayvon thought. When he looked back at the cellphone's screen, Draco's hittaz had taken Trick down from the showerhead and placed him on his knees. They held him up by his arms while Draco stood behind him, prepared to swing his pipe like a baseball bat. Jayvon's answer to Draco's question would determine whether his father would live or die.

"So,what's up, Bloody Knuckles? Do we have a deal?" Draco scowled.

To Be Continued
BLOODY KNUCKLES 2

My self-published books
**BLOODY KNUCKLES
THE DEVIL WEARS TIMBS 1-7
ME AND MY HITTAZ 1-6
THE LAST REAL NIGGA ALIVE 1-3
A HOOD NIGGA'S BLUES
A SOUTH-CENTRAL LOVE AFFAIR**

My books published under LDP
**BURY ME A G 1-5
THE DOPEMAN'S BODYGUARD 1-2
FEAR MY GANGSTA 1-5
THESE SCANDALOUS STREETS 1-3
THE REALEST KILLAZ 1-3
THE LAST OF THE OG'S 1-3
A GANGSTA'S EMPIRE 1-4
GOD BLESS THE TRAPPERS 1-3**

Coming Soon
**BLOODY KNUCKLES 2
THERE'S NO PLACE IN HEAVEN FOR
THUGS
THEY MADE ME AN ANIMAL**

Milton Keynes UK
Ingram Content Group UK Ltd.
UKHW050824290924
1898UKWH00024B/82